WESTERN SHORT STORIES FROM THE GREAT NORTHWEST

Charles M. Harris

WESTERN SHORT STORIES FROM THE GREAT NORTHWEST

SYNOPIS

A Pinkerton agent rides into Mount Vista just as the sun is going down and is confronted by three incompetent bank robbers whose getaway plan involves leaving the body of a stranger at the scene of the robbery. He is chosen to be that stranger. Avoiding the humiliation of such an inglorious death, he proceeds in his quest to capture a former Wells Fargo employee who has robbed a large sum of money left at his employer's office overnight. Information gathered indicates the robber is now in the Mount Visa area. He must face the Wells Fargo robber and his hired gun and confront a mysterious and difficult woman he meets in Mount Vista.

A small man in stature and limited in experience wanted badly to be a law enforcement officer. His father, concerned with that choice, agreed to ask his friend, the marshal, to hire his son as an unpaid apprentice for one year. If his son was not by then sure that he liked the work and could do the job, he would enroll in college. If he did like the work, his father would support him in his efforts to pursue law enforcement as a career. The young man found the work challenging and extremely interesting and could not wait for the year to end.

Arron Begley, a huge, red-headed bank robber upon being released from prison was admonished by the warden that he should give up bank robbing as a career unless he can find a way to become invisible because his physical appearance regardless of a mask will always identify him as the robber. He found a way to become invisible and, upon his release from prison, formed a new gang to rob the bank in Deadwood. During the robbery he shot a bank customer and a member of his gang who tried to help the customer. The gang fled to their nearby hideout but Begley was subsequently captured and the young member of the gang, now in prison, agreed to testify against Begley. The problem: how to get the witness safely back to Deadwood for Begley's trial.

AMENDS

Kerk Holden, as a teenager, worked for his bosses at their livery and also assisted them by holding their horses during occasional bank robberies. On the final and fatal robbery in which his bosses were killed, Kerk was able to escape and make his way to Montana where he joined the army in its battle with the Indians. Upon leaving the army, Kerk headed for Laramie in search for a place where he could start over and make amends for his past. On his way he stopped at a ranch to refill his canteen. There he filled up his canteen and started making amends.

A BITTER HOMECOMING

Rex Todd, in his final year of public school, was forced into a fight with the class bully. Rex unexpectedly won. The embarrassment caused to the bully by the defeat, and by the bully's brother's obvious and public humiliation because of it, caused the bully to commit suicide. The bully's brother, Ezra, blamed Rex and swore revenge. After graduation, Rex joined the army and was sent to Montana where he fought Indians. Because of his ability to anticipate the enemy's action, he advanced rapidly. Upon his discharge, he bought a ranch several miles from his hometown but his only contact with it was through his sister. He received a wire from her advising him that she needed his help. He left immediately.

Deputy Matt Harding was returning from a personal trip to Helena heading back to Deadwood. The stage driver had been fighting heavy winds for the last several miles and now snow made an appearance. With relief, the stage driver and his passengers pulled up to the stage waystation and disembarked. They found the Deadwood stage going in the opposite direction had also arrived and took refuge. When the passengers from both stages gathered around a large table for dinner, a note was delivered to the deputy. The note advised that one of the passengers within the hour would be murdered and another passenger would be the murderer. He had a short time to decide which was which and time was running out.

Ben Hatch, a former lawman, was often referred to as "Cobra" because his draw was so lethal. Since he retired from law enforcement, young guns often challenge him to draw against them hoping if they happened to win, Ben's reputation would automatically pass to them. He had killed two such opponents within the last ninety days and wanted to stop this madness. He decided to try a new town and a new name. Things were going well until an unexpected situation brought the problem back to his doorstep. Another young man, another death. He could leave town again or he could try something different. He chose the latter.

reconvened and, in the defendant's absemce, found him guilty and wanted to hang him on the spot. Matt Harding convinced them the situation was not as it appeared.

Hinkle and Holland, Pinkerton agents, were sent to Johnson County, Wyoming, the site of a deadly range war between the large cattle owners on one side and the small cattle owners and farmers on the other. The issue was grazing rights on government land. That war has finally ended. Pinkerton has been advised that one of its previous employees, Tom Horn, is back in the area and the local citizens fear a modified version of the previous conflict may arise between cattlemen and sheep ranchers. Pinkerton is embarrassed by its previous employment of Horn who turned out to be a ruthless killer and has sent its agents to find Horn and convince him to go somewhere else. They run into opposition from some cowboys but are able to overcome that and locate Horn. Fate steps in and solves their problem.

Two men were deputies in the same marshal's office and became very good friends. At some point, however, they both left law enforcement; one married and became a rancher while the other hired out his gun. They were both recognized as extremely fast and accurate. They lost touch for a while and then circumstances caused them to come together again. Their friendship was greatly tested.

A SOMEWHAT BETTER PLAN

Greg Harvey rode hard to reach Mount Vista before the Montana mid-November darkness and colder temperatures set in for the day. He just made it. He tied his horse in front of the Vista Saloon, across the street from the bank which was still open as evidenced by its lamps shining through the windows. The only person he noticed on the street was a man standing at the side of the saloon trying to keep out of the wind.

The man, a scruffy appearing character, approached Greg with a revolver in his hand. The man was about five feet six and perhaps weighed 130 pounds but his revolver was standard size. Even a small man with a large gun can be dangerous. The man whispered something Greg couldn't hear.

Greg asked, "What did you say?"

"Listen carefully," said the man. "Yer life depends on it. Git back on yer horse and put yer hands on the saddle horn or I'll shoot ya fer sure."

"Is there a reason for this command?

"Yes there is and I'll tell ya because ya need to know. Soon my brothers will come out the bank, get on their horses and ride like blazes up the street behind ya. Ya'll charge out a' here on yer horse and join 'em."

"I suppose your brothers will be carrying bank money."

1

"That's the plan."

"If I catch them, do I get your share?"

"That's not the plan."

Greg asked, "Why was I chosen for this honor?"

"Because ya don't live here an' yer not known."

"Let me guess. As I race to join your brothers, you shoot me. When the law finds the body of a stranger shot during the getaway, it will be assumed none of the robbers are local so you and your brothers will have nothing to worry about. Is that it?"

"Yep, smart ain't it? And I thought of it by myself. Joe, he's in the bank with Silas, my other brother, always says. 'Luke, all yer ideas are stupid and will never work.' He'll like this one though."

"What's Joe's plan?"

"Not much really. We rob the bank when it's gettin' dark so it'll be hard to track us. After a while we slip back into town in time for supper. If the law happen to come by askin' about the robbery, we'll welcome them in fer coffee. My plan will keep 'em from even askin.'"

"How'd you know a stranger would come along?"

"I didn't and that's the beauty of my plan. I made it up as soon as ya pulled up to the hitchin' rail. Joe will like that. Without ya comin', I'd justa been a lookout."

"A lookout should be in front of the bank keeping watch on the marshal's office to see if the law has been alerted."

"It's too cold fer that."

"You certainly plan well. I bet you could come up with a plan for me to get out of this mess."

"No, I don't think so. There ya are on yer horse less than ten feet away from me with yer hands on the saddle horn and me gonna shoot if ya make a wrong move. I don't see no way out for ya."

"What happens to your plan if you have to shoot me before your brothers come out of the bank?"

He seemed puzzled by the question. "I guess no plan's perfect. Ya wouldn't make me shoot just to mess up my plan, would ya?"

"No, no. I wouldn't want to mess up your really good plan."

Actually Greg had a plan of his own, certainly not foolproof. The test wasn't whether his plan was perfect, it was whether it had a better chance of saving his life than letting Luke's plan play out. Instead of rushing off on his horse to follow the robbers and be shot by Luke, Greg planned to simply fall off his horse. He needed to divert Luke's attention. Since Luke didn't appear to be a genius, fooling him shouldn't prove too difficult.

Greg looked over towards the bank which was slightly behind Luke's right shoulder. "Guess we'll know what Joe thinks of your plan in a minute. Your brothers are coming out of the bank now."

As expected, Luke turned around. Greg used the saddle horn to help propel himself off the horse while keeping the animal's body between himself and Luke. By the time he felt the ground under him, Greg had his revolver in his hand and quickly positioned himself so he could see Luke through his horse's legs.

Luke turned back just in time to see Greg drop below his horse's body. He wasn't sure what to do. If he shot a man on the ground, it might look like murder and he'd hang. On the other hand, the man on the ground knew of Luke's involvement in the robbery and he would likely hang for that anyway. He decided to shoot the man and think of an excuse later. He started walking toward Greg's horse.

From between the horse's legs, Greg saw Luke walking in his direction but could only see him from the waist down. When Luke started to bend down in order to better see under the horse, Greg could wait no longer. He shot Luke in the groin. Luke's gun dropped to the ground and almost immediately Luke also fell with his hands covering his injury and rolled back and forth in agony. Luke alternated cursing the day Greg was born and begging him to fetch a doctor.

Hearing the shot, a local rancher ventured out of the saloon and was sent for medical help.

At that moment, the bank doors slammed open and two men came rushing out. They looked identical to Luke. They jumped on their horses and raced down the street near Greg. Greg couldn't let the robbers just ride away but, not wanting to kill them, he shot their horses. The riders sailed through the air to hard landings. One was trying to get up until he saw Greg's gun pointed at him. The other lay there moaning.

The marshal and a deputy came running up from their office several buildings away as two men came out of the bank.

"You with the gun," shouted the marshal, "what's going on?"

"Your bank has just been robbed. These two on the ground are the robbers. Luke, their lookout, is about to be treated by the doctor over near the saloon."

"Marshal, we didn't rob no bank," said Joe. "Tell 'im, Silas."

Silas said nothing, just frowned and seemed confused as to what to say.

Joe repeated, "Silas, tell the marshal we didn't rob no bank."

'Joe, it's truly hard to lie when the bank's money fell out yer pocket."

"I'm Greg Henry. All I did was stop to have a drink in your saloon." The marshal shook his head.

"Stranger, you've encountered Joe, Simon and Luke Renfro perhaps the most inept criminals who ever hoped to commit a crime. What's your story?"

Greg related the events leading up to the shooting.

"Luke planned to make me ride after his brothers and then shoot me. By finding a dead stranger involved in the getaway, Luke thought this would make you think the robbers weren't local."

Silas spoke to Joe. "Luke's plan was dumb since neither of us wore masks an' Jerome knows us."

Joe came to Luke's defense, "Silas, we intended to wear masks but ya forgot yer bandana and it wouldn't help if I wore one."

Silas responded, "I told ya I didn't forget; Sarah washed my bandana and it wasn't dry. I won't wear no wet bandana."

The marshal turned to the young man from the bank, "Jerry, what happened in the bank?"

"Marshal, you won't believe it. Just before closing, Mr. Rivers was back in the manager's office going over the day's accounts. I was making a final count preparing to close my station when Joe and Simon came charging in with revolvers in their hands. Joe rushed up to me and said, 'Jerome, give me some money'.

"I was so amused I decided to correct him. I told him he wasn't there for an allowance so he should say he wanted all the money. After considering it a minute, he said that's what he meant. I told him the answer was no. He asked how I could say no when he had a gun pointed at my head. I told him I knew he wouldn't shoot me. He said I was probably right but if I didn't give him all the money he'd hit me with his gun barrel so hard it'd hurt plenty. That I believed.

"I counted out two hundred dollars and handed it to him. He yelled that wasn't all the money.

'Simon said take it, it was more than they planned to get anyway. I decided to sweeten the pot to get rid of them so I asked if Luke was outside. Simon answered that he was but they wouldn't let him come in. They decided to remove their bullets before entering the bank so they wouldn't accidently hurt me. Luke refused saying he'd never remove his bullets so they made him stay outside. I counted out an extra hundred and handed it to Joe. I told him it was for Luke.

He told me he'd take the money but they probably wouldn't give Luke a full share.

"I told them they'd better go because I'd have to tell the manager they robbed the bank. Joe said that was alright since no one would believe me. I asked why. He told me to be reasonable. I would say they robbed the bank and he and Simon would say they didn't. It would be two against one so who would anyone believe?

"Marshal, I was astounded. For a minute, I saw some logic in Joe's statement."

From his position still on the ground, Joe lifted his head and responded, "Thank ya'. Jerome."

The marshal spoke to Joe, "By Luke's planning to kill the stranger, the crime is more serious and you'll be in prison a long time."

Joe complained since he and Simon went into the bank practically unarmed and begged the marshal to go shoot Luke. Everyone thought he was joking.

Greg ventured back into the cold to find a stall for his horse and a room for himself. He had an early meeting with an old friend.

***

Greg walked into the restaurant thirty minutes late. He looked across the room and saw the 250-pound, six-foot four frame of his friend waiting for him at a table near the window. Greg spent a restless night contemplating how close he came to being murdered by the dumbest crook in Mount Vista. He hoped the people back at the agency never heard of this.

His friend, Billy Radcliff, and he had joined the agency together. Billy married about three years ago. His wife convinced him to leave the job after an agent was killed taking a robber into custody. A week ago Greg contacted Billy to set up this meeting. He walked over to the table where Billy waited.

"Billy, I think you've lost five ounces."

"And I think you've become more pleasant. By the way, a deputy was in here earlier and told us a tall tale in which a stranger was almost killed by the least able criminal around. Could that have been you?"

"Only if it doesn't get back to Pinkerton. I don't understand it. Everyone seems to like the Renfro brothers in spite of their questionable behavior."

"The Renfro brothers are hard working men who do day labor no one else wants to do. They're necessary. Everyone hopes they don't go to prison. Anyway, what do you wish to talk to me about?"

"Shortly after you left Pinkerton, the Wells Fargo Express Office in Helena was held up.

The office was holding a large sum of money overnight intended for shipment the next day. They had three guards on duty, one inside with the manager and two outside. Because the only rear entrance was an especially heavy door and well secured from the inside, the two outside guards stood at each front corner so they could watch down both sides of the building.

"The inside man, Wes Elliot, had been with the company for five years and was well trusted.

It turned out the money was more tempting than preserving his reputation. He knew a character in Helena for some time and arranged to meet him. Wes promised his old friend, Homer Yates, $500 if he'd deliver a horse to a designated spot three hundred feet behind the Wells Fargo office at a prearranged time. Unfortunately,

Wes had a little too much to drink with Homer and divulged that he wanted the money from the robbery to buy a thousand-acre ranch here in the Powder River Basin where he could live the life of a gentleman rancher.

"Wes, being the senior employee, assigned himself as the inside guard. Shortly before the horse was to arrive, Wes, at gunpoint, made the manager open the safe, took its contents, and then hit the manager over the head with his revolver rendering him unconscious.

"He quietly opened the back door and carried the money outside and silently closed the door. He then walked the 300 feet to the waiting horse careful that the building blocked the view of the guards.

Homer wanted to be paid immediately but Wes suggested they get some distance away from the Wells Fargo guards. After they'd ridden about a quarter of a mile, Wes pulled his revolver and said to Homer, 'Old friend, I talked too much during our meeting.' He then shot Homer with the bullet entering his chest just above the heart.

"Instead of falling off his horse as Wes anticipated, Homer slumped over the horse's neck and the horse started running toward the Wells Fargo office. Wes took off in the other direction. By the time Homer reached the Wells Fargo office his horse had almost stopped. One of the outside guards saw the rider was in distress and took him over to Doc Simpson's office.

"The marshal was summoned and asked Homer who shot him. Homer responded, 'The same man who just held up the Wells Fargo office.'

"When the outside guards didn't know of the robbery, Homer knew he was in trouble. If he knew of the robbery before anyone else, he either committed it or was involved.

"In exchange for telling the prosecutor what he knew about Wes, Homer wanted no charges against him since all he did was deliver a horse. The prosecutor refused and Homer refused to cooperate and was sentenced to ten years in prison. We were hired to find Wes and, if possible, the money. Since there is a new prosecutor, I went to him and asked whether he'd make a deal with Homer to get the man who actually committed the robbery. He agreed and authorized me to talk to Homer on his behalf.

"I went to the prison and offered Homer a deal that if he gave me sufficient information to arrest Wes and then testified against him, he'd be released.

"He accepted and told me the man's name was Wes Elliot and he was about your size. Further, he had a bad scar on his right cheek. Most importantly, he told me Wes planned to buy a large ranch here in the Powder River Basin with the stolen money.

"We expected Wes to change his name so we concentrated on sales of large ranches here in the valley shortly after the robbery. We think we've found him. If so, his new name is Robert Dowdy and his ranch is few miles from here. Do you know him?"

"I know of him. He came here a little after I did but we haven't formally met. We both go to the monthly breeder's auction so I've seen him there. His height and weight match but I don't know about the scar since he now wears a full beard. Tomorrow is another breeder's auction if you want to check him yourself.

"Now let me explain why I didn't ask you to stay at the ranch during your visit. My wife's sister is staying with us. It's not that we don't have sufficient room, it's because I didn't want to expose you to Alley. She's nothing like my wife or my wife's other sister, Anna, who has a dress shop in Helena. Alley hates lawmen and soldiers and she'll tell you why so I shouldn't spoil the mystery. I first met Alley when she was just out of her teens. She was the most beautiful woman I've ever seen and a real pleasure to be around."

"What happened to her?"

"The Battle of the Little Big Horn. Her husband, Jake, was assigned to Custer. When she learned he had been killed and worse, mutilated, she blamed him for leaving her a young, childless widow. She wanted a baby and a family very much."

"Maybe it was a blessing that she didn't get pregnant."

"Whatever you do, don't tell her that. My wife insists you come to dinner tonight; a short exposure to Alley might not be too bad. Six o'clock if you still have the nerve."

"I'll see you then."

***

Greg arrived for dinner just before six and Billy, after introducing him to Alley, retreated to the kitchen to assist his wife in preparing dinner.

"I see why Billy said you're the most beautiful woman in the world."

"Why would he say that?"

"Maybe because it's true."

"You men, you're all flatterers. Billy says you are a lawman."

"Actually I work for the Pinkerton Detective Agency. We do occasionally bring bad men to justice."

"Why?"

"If rustlers, robbers, even murderers could operate without restraint this land could not be settled. No one would move here to build towns, operate farms or ranches, or raise families.

Someone has to hold criminals accountable."

"But why you?"

"Because I'm willing and I'm good at it?"

"And because danger thrills you?"

"The work is sometimes dangerous but rarely life threatening. Shootouts with a criminal seldom happen. I take it you don't like lawmen."

"I don't like the chances they take without considering the risks to their wives."

"I have no wife. Does that matter?"

"I suppose you should be able to risk your own life if no one else is affected. My husband was in the army and risked his life for no reason at all. He died leaving me a widow without children. His risk was unfair to the family we might have had."

"Was he in the army when you married him?"

"No. We had small ranch when were newlyweds but an extremely harsh winter killed off most our herd. Jake had to find work in order to build up our stock. The only work he could find was the army and we agreed to only one enlistment. He didn't complete it."

"It seems responsible of him to find another source of income to support his family. If you're so able to dismiss him so easily, why'd you marry him?"

"I truly don't know."

"Was it fair for you to want to have child while Jake was in the army? As much as I love the west, I have to admit that health care here is not what it is back east."

"What would civilization be if women didn't have babies, even here in the west. Besides, it should be a woman's choice if she wants have a baby. You have no wife so you don't know a woman's need to have a child."

"On that you may be right but you're wrong in thinking your husband wasn't thinking about you when he went to the Big Horn."

"Why do you say that? A bunch of men went hunting Indians and they found too many and were killed. What am I missing?"

"Let me tell you. I suppose a good place to start would be the 1868 Treaty of Laramie. It brought temporary peace to the entire area. But there were disputes and the treaty was eventually ignored."

"I don't want a lecture on a treaty that was broken. The important thing is that we lost the battle of the Big Horn but we now have peace with the Indians anyway. Doesn't that prove my husband's sacrifice was meaningless?"

"No. Following Custer's defeat, the War Department sent in a very large number of soldiers to complete the work begun by Custer and his men. The Indian leaders were killed, captured or fled to Canada and the braves returned to the reservation. That is why we have peace today.

"You should realize that valor doesn't depend on winning or losing. It's having a commitment to a worthy cause and a willingness to sacrifice in order to achieve it. Your husband and those with him were committed to protect the ranchers, the farmers, the wagon trains and others by forcing the Indians back to the reservations. They gave everything for you, for Billy and Abby, for me and for so many others. These men are my heroes. I am offended that you refuse to honor and respect their courage and commitment.

"I see I have offended you and since a guest should never offend his host's family, I'll be leaving. Thank your sister for the invitation and tell Billy I'll see him tomorrow at the auction."

"I don't expect you to leave."

"It's something I expect of myself," he said as he moved toward the door.

Her sister, Abby, had been listening from the kitchen and came out to check on Alley.

"Are you all right?" She asked.

"He's impossible. I see why no woman would ever marry him."

"Oh, he was married."

"He told me he has no wife."

"He doesn't now. She and their baby died in childbirth."

"Well at least she was able to make the choice."

"It really wasn't her choice. She wanted to wait a while so she and Greg could have some time together. Greg was the one who wanted a family and talked her into it. Grief and guilt are horrible companions. Greg has lived with both for far too long."

Alley seemed stunned. "My God, Abby. What have I done, what have I become? How could you and Billy put up with me? I won't be joining you for dinner. I need to do some thinking and that won't be easy."

With that, Alley retreated to her room.

In a few minutes Billy returned from bringing in firewood.

"I saw Greg leave. Did you see any claw marks on him?"

"No, I think Alley is the one injured. But, Billy, I think we may have my sister back."

***

Greg arrived at the breeder's auction a half hour early. The bidders were already there examining the bulls set for auction. He was surprised to see Abby and Alley sitting in a carriage talking to Billy. He rode over to Billy, dismounted, and nodded to the women, "Ladies."

Alley responded, "Greg, I would like to talk to you before you leave." He looked at her inquisitively.

13

"Please," she said.

"Of course."

Greg then spoke to Billy, "Is he here?"

"Yes, that's him by the railing with the brown hat."

"He doesn't appear armed."

"He is if you take into account the shorter man standing next to him. That's Buddy Hayman. Dowdy brought him up from Texas about six months ago. I think it was insurance against this day happening. Dowdy has introduced Hayman as his foreman but he knows nothing about tending cattle. Buddy claims to be the fastest gun in the area. Either he is or he's sold himself so well that no one here has challenged him and that's about the same thing."

"Well, I have a job to do."

Greg approached the man calling himself Dowdy, "Mr. Elliot, my name is Greg Harvey.

A federal judge in Helena has issued a warrant for your arrest for robbing the Wells Fargo Express Office in Helena and the attempted murder of your partner. The United States Marshal in Helena has named me a special deputy to bring you in. Turn around and put your hands behind your back."

"My name's Robert Dowdy."

"We both know your name. Now turn around."

"Buddy, this man has implied I'm a thief. Earn your money."

Hayman removed his outer coat and hung it over his saddle horn."

Hayman nodded at Greg, "Harvey, it's too late to apologize. The marshal's here if you want to ask him to make me behave or you can just walk away but either way I'll find you later and kill you."

"Bullet holes in the back make self-defense a difficult claim."

"I see you understand the situation."

Greg removed his outer coat and handed it to Billy who had walked up.

"Mr. Hayman, I have no warrant for your arrest. You should really stay out of this."

"I can't; ya insulted my boss."

"I'm curious, how much is Elliot paying you to die for him?"

"Why do you think you can beat me?"

"Because I practiced more in my youth."

"Let's see if it made a difference." They both went for their guns.

A casual observer would say it looked as though each revolver came out of its holster at the same instant and that the sounds of the explosions propelling the bullets from the barrels were contemporaneous. But when time is measured in fractions of a second, both sight and sound can be misleading. Greg's bullet slammed into Hayman's heart just as Hayman was completing his trigger-pull causing his bullet to veer harmlessly to the right. Hayman fell to his knees, looked at Greg and said in a whisper, "Not nearly enough." He fell forward on his face, dead.

Greg handcuffed Elliot as the marshal walked up.

"That's the best gunfight I've ever seen. Not much difference between you. Can I do anything?"

"Thanks for staying out of it. If you will, I'd like you to hold Elliot in your jail tonight and I'll pick him up early for the trip back to Helena."

"Glad to. He's a big man. Won't it be dangerous to take him all that way alone? You might get tired or careless and he could overpower you."

"I have my method, Marshal."

"Greg, I've had a lot of people ask about the Renfro brothers. They like them. They expect them to do dumb things but because they are necessary we make allowances. They clean the stables, cut fire wood, do many jobs most men don't want to do. If the men are gone long, the churches and the families will have to chip in to help their families. What do you say?"

"I say you have an odd town."

"No, Gregg, just a few odd people."

"Marshal, Luke's too dumb to be very dangerous. I'd be happy with three months' probation if a condition is that Luke can't have any bullets in his gun. What does the bank say?"

"Since they didn't lose any money, they don't care. With your agreement, the prosecutor will go with probation."

The marshal walked off with his prisoner and Greg walked over to the carriage.

"Thanks for coming over, Greg. I want to apologize for my flippant remarks about only women having an interest in the decision to have a child. I can see that could have been hurtful."

"It was a long time ago and I've moved on."

"I wonder. I also considered your remarks about how I failed to properly respect my husband. You were right and I'm ashamed. I was blinded by self-pity. I realize now that Jake didn't die because of what he did, he died because of who he was. Fighting the Indians is not why Jake died, it's only how he died. He died because he felt an obligation to do his duty and he did so without pause and without looking for someone else to do it for him. He was a reliable, dependable man and that's why I loved him and that's why I married him.

"I saw the same qualities in you today. You didn't want to face that gunfighter. You tried to talk him out of it. When it was apparent he would stand between you and your duty, you immediately stepped forward. You didn't ask anyone to intervene on your behalf. You were dependable and responsible. I admire that. Greg, I like you and I believe that feeling might grow if it had an opportunity and if . . ."

"If what?"

"If you weren't so afraid of a woman of child bearing age."

"I'm not afraid . . ."

"Of course you are. How many women have you called on during the two years your wife has been gone? Anyway, I'm moving to Helena next week to give Abby and Billy a break and to help my sister in her dress shop. I'll be there if you'd like to call."

"I still work for Pinkerton."

"I know what you do and, more importantly, I know who you are. Now I have the wisdom to know the difference."

"Alley, I'm not going to Helena until tomorrow. May I call on you tonight?"

"Oh yes, Greg. Please do."

Abby spoke up, "Come to supper at six and this time stay for the meal." She turned the carriage and headed back to the ranch.

Greg stood there, smiling, and watched them go.

MOLASSES

Harry Allen was a twenty year old still living with his parents and working on the family ranch. Most would describe him as an average person, at least in Ridge City, Montana a few miles southwest of Virginia City. His height of five foot seven and a weight of a hundred forty pounds limited his opportunities, at least in his chosen profession of law enforcement.. His father, a very successful rancher, was a large man who was sympathetic to his son's problem. He knew Harry wasn't happy on the ranch. He offered to set Harry up in business along main street. But Harry wanted to be a law enforcement officer.

"Harry," the father once told his son, "You're smart so why not go to college? You could be a teacher. We always need teachers and it would make your mom happy if you stayed around here."

"Dad, you've made that offer before. Going to college would be about as exciting as ranching."

"All of your friends say you are the slowest draw of any of them. What happens if you are in a saloon one evening breaking up a fight and one of the cowboys says, 'deputy, I think I'm faster than you. Let's go outside and let me prove it.'"

"Dad, that just doesn't happen, or it doesn't happen with any frequency. The O.K. Coral fight, probably the most famous gunfight, was not a gunfight between two men. It was a mob shootout involving handguns and rifles. One man didn't 'draw' against another. They simply started shooting.

"I talked to Marshal Zimmerman and he says he's heard of no Montana marshal ever being challenged to draw his gun. And once my gun is in my hand, everyone will tell you I'm extremely accurate."

"I've also talked to the marshal, you know he's a good friend, and he suggests that you intern with him for a year to see if you really want to be a peace officer. A lot of the work can be quite boring. And how would you react if you had to kill a man?"

"The exciting part to me would simply be being there to lend assistance to anyone who needs it. If I'm never called upon to draw my revolver or get physical with a large, drunken cowboy that would be good also. I admit the answer as to how I'd react to killing a person is unknown. But the marshal has been in law enforcement for over ten years and he's never killed anyone."

"Okay, Son, here's the deal. Intern with the marshal for one year. If you still want to be in law enforcement, I'll support your wish. If not, It's off to college you go."

They struck the deal.

Ridge City is a great town. People are friendly, helpful, and generally compassionate. Except when it comes to nicknames. For example, Robin Yates, a classmate during their first year of school, was a slow learner. His classmates, regrettably he among them, called him "Dummy." That is until the teacher heard someone call him that.

"Children," she said, "You'll get one warning and this is it. If I hear such cruelty again you'll be in trouble."

"But, Miss Reams, Robin doesn't mind. He just laughs when we say it," justified one of the smarter students.

"What else can he do, Miles? Robin does have some trouble with his homework now but he'll improve. What he also has is a characteristic that warrants a better nickname. Robin always appears happy. Why not call him "Happy." It is accurate and, at the same time, inoffensive."

So Robin became "Happy" and even though it wasn't apparent if it pleased him, it certainly pleased the teacher and that pleased all of the students.

Harry wished he'd had Miss Reams in high school. His nickname didn't come along until his last year. Almost all the boys in class lived on farms or on ranches. At about twelve, they were taught to use a rifle so they could hunt with their fathers. At sixteen, because of where they lived and the nature of how things were, they were also permitted to own handguns and practice under the supervision of a parent. Harry always won the turkey shoot at the annual Thanksgiving day rifle contest. Once they learned to shoot a handgun accurately, the boys decided to learn to fast draw. The others soon learned very well; Harry didn't. His friends agreed that once he got his pistol out of his holster, his adversary would be in trouble but by then he'd have been shot three times. They said he was as slow as molasses. Because it was an accurate description of his draw, it stuck.

Marshal Zimmerman had one deputy, Burt Owens, and that was all the budget would allow. When Harry began his unpaid internship he did such things as keep the office presentable, keep track of supplies, and be responsible for the wanted posters that would arrive occasionally.

He would choose the posters which involved a crime committed close to Ridge City and hang that poster on a bulletin board just outside the marshal's office. Others he would place in a file and leave on the marshal's desk until he and the deputy had an opportunity to look them over. He then put them in storage for later reference. One day he placed the poster of Hank Ellis on the board. He and his gang of six robbed a bank in Virginia City. Although it happened three weeks earlier, the poster arrived early that morning. The teller was killed. There was a reward of three thousand dollars being offered, dead or alive, for Ellis. Nothing was said about his gang members, perhaps only Ellis had been identified. Three thousand dollars was a great deal of money when "forty dollars a month and keep" was a normal wage for cowboys in the area.

An assignment Harry gave himself was that at the end of the day he'd go by one of the saloons, nurse a beer, and see if any strangers were in town. He thought this kind of information might be helpful to a lawman.

It was slightly after five when Harry entered Big Ben's saloon. The crowd hadn't yet arrived. The barkeep, Sid O'Neal, a saloon girl named Ruby, Billy Evans, the piano player who was setting up to perform, three regulars from a local ranch, and a clerk from the general store were the only ones there. That is, except for two strangers sitting at separate tables and showing no indication of familiarity with each other.

Harry pulled his gun and faced one of the strangers he recognized from the morning's wanted posters. It was Hank Ellis, the bank robber and killer from Virginia City. He had no idea who the other stranger was so he asked his name and whether he was he with Ellis. He said he was Milo Perkins and had just come in for a drink and that he had never seen the man before. Everyone in the saloon agreed they came in separately.

"Mr. Ellis, stand up and drop your gun belt."

Ellis looked at him, "How'd ya know."

"Your wanted poster came in today. Looks exactly like you."

"Kid, yer not even wearin' a star and yer far too young to be any danger to me. Go home while ya' can."

With that, Ellis stood, squared up, and held his hand about six inches above his revolver giving Harry a chance to withdraw.

"Ellis, I see your wearing a .45 Smith & Wesson. Billy the Kid liked that gun. But yours has a pearl handle. How many notches do you have?"

21

"If ya' don't leave now, there'll be one more."

Harry moved the barrel of his revolver slightly and fired. The bullet ricocheted off the pearl-handled .45 and spread pearl fragments across the floor.

"If you don't drop what's left of your gun and head toward the marshal's office, the next bullet will center your chest."

Ellis reluctantly unbuckled his gun belt and let it fall to the floor as he headed toward the door.

"Mr. O'Neal," Harry said nodding at the other stranger, "please cover my back until I get to the marshal's office."

"You bet," O'Neal said and reached under the bar and pulled out a short barrel shotgun and placed it on the counter beside him.

* * *

Harry entered the jail and informed Marshal Zimmerman that he was delivering him a present he found in the saloon.

"It's Hank Ellis, a robber and a murderer from Virginia City. His picture's on the board outside."

"Put him in a cell while I check the board."

"I should tell you there was another stranger in town but they didn't seem to be together and we don't have a poster on the other one so I didn't arrest him."

"That's good, Harry. We can't arrest anyone for just being a stranger in town. I don't want to hold Ellis here any longer than necessary so I'm going to the telegraph office and wire the marshal of Virginia City to send someone tomorrow to pick 'em up."

"Marshal, do you want me to stay with him tonight?"

"Naw, that's my job. Just stay with him a few minutes. I'm not married so there's no problem with me coming down here and taking the other cell. I'm also going to tell the marshal to put yer name in for the reward. Harry, that'll make you too wealthy to become a deputy."

* * *

The next morning, Harry arrived at the jail at eight o'clock. To his amazement, Zimmerman's horse was not in front. Harry was apprehensive because he knew a prisoner was inside and the marshal would not leave him alone. He drew his weapon and cautiously opened the unlocked jail.

He saw what appeared to be the marshal laying in the bunk in the second cell. However, the man on the bunk in Ellis' cell looked suspicious. On checking, he found both cells unlocked. He opened the cell occupied by the marshal. His suspicion was justified. The marshal had been killed by a hard blow to the back of his head. In Ellis' cell, he found that some extra pillows had been quickly placed under Ellis' blanket. He left the jail without bothering to lock it. After all, the horses had left the barn.

Seeing Bill Rice, the shopkeeper next door, he informed him of what happened and, since there now was no marshal, asked him to notify the mayor. He waited in the jail until the mayor arrived.

It was twenty minutes later when the Mayor got there and with him were Clay Wrigley, owner the Ridge City Bank, Harvey Simpson, editor of the local newspaper, and Wilbur Abbott, owner of the hardware store.

"I'm sorry it took so long, Harry, but since we now have no marshal, I thought it wise to bring along the other members of the council. It will take my recommendation and the council's vote to name a new marshal. I just learned that Burt Owens quit as Zimmerman's deputy because the pay was too low. I saw him on the street and asked him to come also. He should be here soon. Perhaps he'll accept the job as temporary marshal since it pays more."

The Mayor went on, "You did the right thing to stay here once you determined the marshal was dead, Harry."

Harry more carefully examined both cells. Burt Owens, the former deputy, came in and casually looked around.

Simpson, the editor, mentally preparing his story for the next issue, asked Owens what he thought happened.

"Well," Owens replied, "I heard young Allen arrested a bad one last night. I'd say Marshal Zimmerman, gettin' more careless as he got older, stood too close to the cell and Ellis was able to reach his gun and the keys and this is what happened."

"Does that sound right to you, Harry?" pursued the editor.

"No, Sir. I never saw the marshal being careless. I think I know who killed Marshal Zimmerman and how and when it probably happened."

"'For someone with no experience as a lawman, that's a amazin' statement," responded Owens with a sneer. "Mayor, if you want me to take over this investigation, get the kid out of my way."

"'Explain your reasoning, Harry," interrupted Clay Wrigley.

"I know how cautious the marshal was. We talked about it on several occasions. Because he was so short-handed, he took extreme steps. Once a prisoner was arrested who posed a serious threat, no one could enter the jail armed. The marshal would be armed with a shotgun. As soon as the prisoner was fed his evening meal, the marshal would lock the jail for the evening. No visits after the prisoner is fed. He'd put the prisoner in one cell and himself in the other with the keys to both cells in his pocket. Even if someone had been able to get into the jail after closing, they'd have found both keys missing and the marshal in the other locked cell. The marshal wouldn't give up the key even if they shot him. The shot would have alerted everyone around with Ellis still in the cell and the shooter desperate to get out of town."

Owens spoke up, "Then tell us how Ellis by hisself was able to get out of his cell and kill the marshal after the jail had been locked for the night."

"Ellis didn't kill the marshal. Milo, the other stranger in the saloon, did. That's the who. When is while Ellis was being fed and that would have been shortly after seven. Most of you know that when a prisoner is in custody, the diner across the street prepares dinners for the marshal and the prisoner and sends Happy over with them. I believe Milo saw Happy with the trays of food heading toward the jail and followed him hoping for an opportunity.

"Since the prisoner had not yet been fed, the jail would not have been locked. The procedure was that when Happy opened the door and entered with the food, he'd kick the jailhouse door shut behind him. Then the marshal would order the prisoner to the back of the cell. He'd motion Happy to come over with the food. He'd have his tray placed on his desk and open the cell door wide enough for Happy to put the prisoner's tray on the floor.

"Happy should've made sure the jail door closed all the way but because it was a heavy door sometimes it didn't completely close or possibly Milo was close enough behind Happy to block the closing with his foot and his action simply wasn't noticed. But I think this was one of those times when the door for whatever reason didn't fully close and Milo was able to silently push it open.

"In any event, the marshal would have been concentrating on the prisoner to make sure he didn't try to grab Happy as a hostage. Milo was able to walk up behind him and land a fatal blow to the back of his head. When Happy started to yell, he did the same to him. Milo then opened the cell doors to let Ellis out and put the marshal in the cell he previously occupied. He did his best to make Ellis' cell look occupied."

"Mayor, the kid is purely guessin' that a second man was involved or that Happy even showed up."

The mayor asked, 'How sure are you there was a second man or that it happened after Happy arrived?'

"Positive. You can see just inside Ellis' cell some food spilled. They tried to clean it up but they didn't do a good job. I cleaned that area myself earlier in the day."

"'If your right, Allen, where's Happy and where're the trays?" pursued Owens.

"Mayor, since you're standing right next to the storage room will you open the door?"

Happy and the trays were inside.

Owens had nothing to say.

Wrigley continued the questioning, "Harry, if they had Ellis out of his cell and two bodies at their feet, why'd they stay around long enough to clean up the mess? If they simply rode off, they'd have a head start to get a long way from here."

"Two reasons. First, they lacked a horse. Milo, of course, had his but Ellis' horse was being held in the livery and it would have been too risky to try to get it. Instead Ellis took the marshal's.

"Second, because they weren't going far anyway. They were concerned that when Happy didn't reappear with the trays, someone from the diner would come to check on him. If they found the cells open and two bodies on the floor, alarms would have sounded and a search immediately started. If there had been an immediate search, the posse may have tracked them to their hideout. However, if the one checking on Happy looked through the jail window and saw two cells occupied, they'd reason Happy for some reason had just gone home after delivering the trays. If a search was delayed for several hours, as it was in this case, it would appear one would be hopeless and none would be undertaken."

Simpson asked, "Why would they need a hideout? You'd expect them to just leave the area."

"We have two members of a gang of six bank robbers in our saloon early last evening and they pretended not to know each other. Why were they here? Was it just to have a drink or were they in town to locate the bank in relation to the marshal's office and find a quick escape route out of town? Remember, we are known all around the area as a small town with a small bank with a big safe with a lot of money. The big safe is needed because at the end of the month the miner's bring their gold nuggets to the bank for overnight storage before placing them on the train to Denver the next morning for the final smelting process. The other four gang members probably waited at the hideout for them. This is the end of the month and I think they plan to rob the bank today, probably just before closing."

Clay Wrigley confirmed, "The gold came in under heavy guard from the mine about thirty minutes ago."

The mayor asked, "If that's the case, Owens, what should we do?"

"'Well, if there's only six of 'em, we get eight 'er ten heavily armed men hidin' out and when six strangers ride into town we blast 'em off their horses."

The mayor pursued the issue, "Harry, what's your view?"

"Marshal Zimmerman was a very smart man and read a lot. He liked to talk to me about the books and articles he read. He particularly liked to read about famous battles, ancient and modern. One of his favorite battles was the Great Northfield Minnesota Raid about ten years ago. He'd read about it in one of those dime novels. The James gang and the Dalton gang and three other outlaws came together to rob the Northfield bank. So as not to arouse suspicion, the gang members rode into town in small groups but made the mistake of wearing linen dusters that some townspeople thought might conceal weapons. They were also riding particularly fine horses that one might expect to be helpful for a fast getaway.

"This aroused suspicions and the townspeople quietly took appropriate positions and waited for confirmation of their concerns. They didn't think it right to shoot e strangers for just wearing fancy coats and riding good horses. When a bank teller refused to open the safe, an outlaw shot him in the head. The outlaws immediately realized this was a grave mistake. Knowing the town would be alerted, the gang rushed toward their horses without any money. They were met with a volley of gunfire. Two outlaws were killed and several others wounded as the gang made its way out of town. A posse was formed and all the gang members, with the exception of Frank and Jesse James, were captured.

"This is Marshal Zimmerman's advice to us from the grave. "Let the robbers enter town but if they attempt to rob the bank, be ready for them.

"I suggest a modified version of Owens' plan. The difference is that there should be no shooting until we know the strangers are here to rob our bank."

The banker looked at Harry, "I don't want my employees exposed to danger."

"They won't be. The gang killed my friend and I request to be the only one inside the bank when the robbers arrive."

"How will you survive if all six charge into the bank at once?"

"They won't. The robbers usually send one man in first pretending to be a customer. His job will be to take out the bank guard and control the inside of the bank before the rest come in.. About a minute later, the rest will ride up, survey the street to make sure nothing is out of place, hitch their horses close to the bank, and casually enter the bank together to complete the robbery. I'll take care of the advance man and then make sure the rest come in one at time."

"How will you do that?"

"Marshal Zimmerman had another story he liked to tell about a battle that occurred around 500 B.C. It was called the Battle of Thermopylae and was between Persia and Greece. Persia had a huge army going up against a greatly outnumbered Greek force. The problem Persia had was that its army had to go through the pass of Thermopylae in order to reach the Greeks. The Greek leader placed his smaller army which included the 300 Spartans, remembered even now for their valor, in position to block the pass.

"You see, It didn't matter how many men the Persians had, it was how many they could employ against the defending Greeks at the appropriate time. The walls of the pass funneled the Persians into a manageable number for the Greeks' superior archers. The dead bodies of the Persians stacked up in the pass after each charge and caused each later charges to be even more difficult.

"My plan is to narrow the pass — the entry door into the bank— so that only one person at a time can enter. Once they see the futility of proceeding, they will retreat and then it will be up to you."

* * *

Harry positioned himself in the bank so he was behind the door when the gang's point-man arrived. With gun in hand, he ordered him to the floor and handcuffed his wrists behind his back, tied his ankles close together and dragged the man to a spot behind the teller cage. He then stuffed a bank-bag in the outlaw's mouth.

Knowing the rest of the gang would shortly arrive, Harry pulled a heavy chair from the conference room and placed it behind the entry door so the door would open only about a fourth of the way. He tested it and found it satisfactory. He stepped back about ten feet and waited with his gun in hand.

Harry heard horses approach and stop. Men began crossing the wooden walkway to the door. Ellis gave instructions, "Me and Milo will enter first. The rest of you right behind."

Ellis pushed the door but found it would open only part way. He hit the door with his shoulder but it wouldn't move. In frustration, Ellis pushed his left shoulder and his head through the small opening to find the cause of the obstruction. Instead he saw Harry.

"It's that damn kid from the saloon."

When he realized his gun was in his right hand, useless because it was behind the door, he started to withdraw. Harry's bullet dropped him to the floor between the door and doorjamb. Milo, like a lemming, pushed over Ellis and placed his head and shoulder through the same narrow opening but at least held his gun in his left hand. First he looked for the cause of the obstruction and then for the shooter. It was the wrong sequence. Another shot from Harry's gun and a pile began to form at the bank's door.

The gang members outside realized that continuing their effort would not be a good idea and bolted for their horses, firing their guns as they did to discourage anyone coming out onto the street.

From the shooting from all directions around them, they soon realized men were already there.

Clay Wrigley, with a rifle he had not shot for years, was firing from the rooftop of a building directly across from his bank. Walter Abbott, the owner of the hardware store with a revolver in hand, was firing from a second story window in the same building. Simpson was firing from the doorway of his newspaper office a few doors down. The three ranch hands who had been in the saloon the evening before had returned for an early start to a big weekend and were recruited to help defend against a bank robbery. They agreed and were behind a water trough near the bank giving them a ground-level view.

The fear of stopping too soon caused the shooting to go on much longer than necessary. Each gang member in the street outside the bank bore numerous wounds.

Finally, all was quiet.

The three ranch hands stood and looked at the bodies across from them. They had all served in the army during the Indian wars a few years earlier and were hardened by the deaths they witnessed at the time.

One remarked to his friends, "Our side got through this battle with no casualties. A celebration is in order and I'll buy the first round." They headed back to Big Ben's. The mayor met them to give them his thanks and assure them their drinks would be on the city..

The hardware owner returned to his store. Wrigley and Simpson stood looking at the bodies as Henry made his way over the bodies of Ellis and Milo and out of the bank with his lone prisoner.

"Harvey," said Wrigley, "we did a good thing. We saved the life savings of a lot of our neighbors. It would have been hard on them to have no savings when they can no longer work. So why do I feel so bad?"

"Clay, I feel the same way. I think the answer must be that while it's one thing to contemplate killing a man even for a good reason, it's quite another to *have* killed a man regardless of the reason. Even if the killing is justified, the hurt, the doubt is going to linger."

As Harry walked up, he addressed his friends, "I heard you talking about having killed someone. You don't know that you killed anyone. Sure you shot some people but that doesn't mean you killed them. These bodies are riddled with gunshots and you can't tell which is the fatal bullet or from whose gun it came. Your shot may have just wounded the man or hit him after he was dead.

"It's like being on a firing squad where everyone is firing blanks except one and no one knows who had the live ammunition. You simply can't know for sure if you killed anyone."

"Harry," Harvey said with moist eyes, "I appreciate your trying to help. But my concern is less with what I did, than why I did it. I wanted to kill them. I didn't do it totally out of a community obligation. Oh, I'm glad we stopped the robbery. But while I was shooting I kept seeing Happy before me and thought anyone who would kill him didn't deserve to live. I'm afraid I killed them for revenge, perhaps the worst possible reason."

Harry had a prisoner to put in jail and realized someone would have to take charge of the jail and stay with the prisoner until a lawman could be selected. He advised the two council members they needed find the mayor and immediately hire a lawman. He started to walk away.

He heard Wrigley asked after him, "Harry, do you still want to be marshal?"

The answer came quickly, "No. I have no doubt I killed today. The two men in the doorway have one bullet apiece in them. Those are my bullets. I don't want to do it again. Tell the Mayor if he wishes me to stay with the prisoner until he can find a new marshal, he should hurry. I have plans to make for college."

'Harvey," inquired Clay, "What are you going to do now?

"I'm going to the office and write tomorrow's editorial. I don't intend to use names of those of us in the street; we were just local people doing our duty. We were acting for everyone and most, had we had time to gather them, would have stood with us. But I do intend to mention by name Harry Allen. He's the best marshal we never had. He was never officially our marshal and was never on our payroll but he planned our defense and led us through it. His stand at the entrance to the pass would make any Spartan proud."

END

A TRIP ON THE CHEYENE – DEADWOOD STAGE

Aaron Begley knew he wasn't cut out for his chosen profession but he loved the challenge, the excitement, the money. He had to admit, however, that standing six foot six with bright red hair made him conspicuous. Too conspicuous, his prison warden told him, to be a bank robber. The warden delighted in saying, "Even if you wear a mask to obscure your facial features, your red hair and towering presence will give you away every bit as much as if you leave your signature at the scene of the crime. If you're going to continue to rob banks, you'd better become invisible and no one's ever done that."

When he got out of prison, Begley figured out how to become invisible. He formed a new gang to test his theory. He recruited four men plus himself for his first post-prison robbery and chose a Deadwood bank because it was near his family home near Cheyenne Crossing which would make a great hideout. It was his parents ranch until they died.

When they reached the bank timed to be just before closing, Arron, most often called "Red," assigned one gang member to act as lookout and have the horses ready after the robbery.

He sent the other three into the bank to overpower the guard and take control of the customers and employees. These three then put blindfolds on all those in the bank and advised them that if they removed the blindfolds they would be shot. Red was notified when it was time for his entry.

He figured if no one could see him, he was invisible.

One man was assigned to go behind the teller station to grab the money while the other two continued to watch the employees and customers. Red led the manager back into his office where the safe was located and ordered him to remove his blindfold but face only the safe and open it. If he failed to do either he would be killed. Once the safe was opened, Red hit the manager in the back of his head with the butt of his revolver rendering him unconscious. Red removed the money from the safe and retreated from the manager's office to gather his men for departure. But he ran into an obstacle. He stood facing, eye to eye, a customer whose blindfold had slipped down. Red pulled his revolver and pointed it at the customer, "You were told what would happen."

"Red, don't do it," interjected Roy Acres, twenty-year-old and by far the youngest member of the gang as he stepped in front of the customer;" "it wasn't his fault. I didn't tie it right."

Red looked at the young man for a few seconds. "Roy, accepting you into the gang was a big mistake. You'll never make a good bank robber."

With that, Red shot Roy and, when Roy fell out of the way, shot the customer. The gang fled the bank as men started heading in their direction. They avoided the slow-forming posse and made it to their hideout in Cheyenne Crossing, a small community about a dozen miles away. After they put their horses in the barn and entered the house, the man who served as lookout asked what the shooting was all about.

Red explained, "I shot a customer who didn't follow instructions to keep his blindfold on and Roy who tried to help him."

"That's fine, boss, but are you sure they're dead? Roy can identify all of us."

"Henry, I can't imagine they're not dead. I was less than ten feet away when I shot them. But I agree we need to know. I want you to go back into Deadwood, no one can identify you, and just hang out for a while until you find out if they died. We plan to stay here for about a week until things cool down. Come back when you have word."

***

Matt Harding, the chief deputy of Deadwood, had been out of the office when the robbery occurred and was disappointed that a posse had not been formed in time to give meaningful chase. The posse, when it was finally formed, almost immediately lost the outlaws' tracks and Matt knew the marshal who was away on a hunting trip would not be happy.

On learning of the robbery, Matt visited the bank to interview the witnesses. The information gained, although scant, was nevertheless telling. The statements of all the witnesses were consistent, three robbers with bandana masks came into the bank and took control of those inside. They put blindfolds on everyone, employees and customers alike. Although those inside saw the three robbers for a short time, the only description they could give of the outlaws was that they were of average height and weight and that the bandanas obscured their facial features.

They also recounted how one, upset that a customer's blindfold had slipped down, shot him. He also shot a gang member.

So why blindfold everyone in the bank? Matt thought he had the answer. Another robber, probably the leader, had a feature a mask would not hide. For example, he could be four feet tall and weigh two hundred pounds. It's because, Matt reasoned, that a mere mask wouldn't sufficiently hide him that he came in only after the blindfolds were in place. Matt decided to check all wanted posters for someone who might qualify for the extra precaution.

Matt left the bank and proceeded to the clinic where he encountered Dr. Al Allison. Al was not his first name but it was the only name he would divulge.

"Al, how bad is it?"

"Actually good and bad. The young bandito I thought was a goner for sure when they brought him in. Blood everywhere. But the bullet went between his chest and his arm grazing both. A lot of blood but easy to treat. I want to see him in the morning but then you can move him to jail if you want.

"Sid White is another story. The bullet did some extensive internal injuries. I won't know about him for a while."

"Did he say anythin'?"

"Yeah, two things you might find of interest. He described the robber-in-chief as being at least six feet six inches tall with bright red hair and two, he couldn't stop singing the praises of the young robber. Incidentally, his name is Roy Acres. Sid said he'd been loosening his blindfold just a little so he could see underneath it to see what was going on. Unfortunately, he loosened it too much and it slipped down. When the redheaded one saw Sid's blindfold down, he announced Sid would die. The young outlaw stepped between them and took the blame for the loose blindfold saying he hadn't tied it properly. Red shot them both before leaving the bank."

"Do you think I'll be able to talk to Sid?"

"Come by in the morning and you can pick up Roy and perhaps talk to Sid. He still has periods of consciousness."

***

Matt arrived at the clinic about ten the following morning. Since Sid was awake, he talked to him first. Sid repeated the information reported by the doctor and again had high praise for the young outlaw. He was also shown some old wanted posters and picked out the man who shot him.

Matt then approached Roy Acres, highly bandaged but sitting up in bed.

"How do you feel today?"

"Like I've been shot?"

"Who did it?

"Deputy, I've been considering that question. I'm grateful for the care I've received and know I don't deserve it. I realize I must be punished for what I did. In fact, I wish to plead guilty and start paying my debt as soon as possible. But when it comes to names, the gang members were good to me and I won't help you with them. Although I owe nothing to the crazy leader, if I give you his name it may get the others in trouble. Besides, I know the bank customer saw him clearly and I saw you talk to him. My guess is you already have his description."

"More than that; I also have his name. I brought over some old wanted posters and Mr. White picked out Arron Bigley."

"To be honest with you, I didn't know his name, just Red. I doubt the other gang members know his actual name."

Matt waited for Roy to get dressed and walked him to jail.

***

On their way to jail, Matt led Roy past a saloon with several men standing outside.

Questions came from several of the men which Matt answered as they walked past.

"Is this one of the robbers, Deputy?"

"Yep."

"Has he confessed?"

"He doesn't deny bein' one of the robbers."

"Did he give you the names of the gang members?"

"No. He's true to the code, he wouldn't divulge anythin'."

"How's Sid?"

Matt stopped walking and turned to answer the question. "Frank, the news there is not very good. He's in bad shape and the doctor won't know just how bad for a while."

"Could he give a description?"

Matt knew the question would come and decided not to be forthcoming. It might be better if Mr. Begley remained unaware that his identity was known. "I knew Sid's condition should keep me from questionin' him."

Matt then ended the questioning session and led Roy across the street and into the jail.

Roy looked at the deputy and whispered, "Devious."

"Perhaps, but maybe effective."

One of the cowboys standing in the group in front of the saloon who had his hat pulled well down over his head moved away from the saloon, mounted his horse, and headed south out of town. When this man, Henry, arrived at the hideout he was greeted by Red.

"What news do you have?"

"Mostly good. I was in a group of men hanging out in front of the saloon when the deputy led Roy by on the way from the clinic to the jail. I stood in the back with my face mostly covered by my hat. The deputy answered several questions. The most important was that Roy wouldn't give us up. He refused to help in any way."

"Well," said Red, "perhaps there's something good about him after all. What about the man whose blindfold dropped?"

"It looks like he won't make it. The doctor doesn't know now."

"That's good news. I was afraid Roy may have put the law on to us. Tonight we'll go into Cheyenne Crossing to celebrate. I remember the stage way-station had good food and tolerable liquor before I went off to prison."

***

Matt, having written up his brief interview with Sid White and noted his non-interview with Roy Acres, went back into the cell section of the jail to talk to Roy.

"Roy, I promised the doctor I'd take you back today so he can change your bandages. Are your wounds botherin' you?"

"Not too much, Deputy. By the way, if you wanted Red not to know you were aware of his name, you handled the questioning just right. One of his gang was in that crowd of men in front of the saloon and I saw him leave as soon as we passed."

"Now you tell me. But it might still be helpful."

Matt walked out of the cell section and back to his desk. Why, he asked himself, would Red send a gang member back into Deadwood? The most logical reason is that although Red must have believed he killed Roy and Sid, he had second thoughts. If they weren't dead they'd pose a big threat to him. Now that he knows that Roy won't talk and Sid may not live, he probably feels much better.

Matt remembered vaguely Red's trial which was held in Deadwood about three years ago. It seems that Red grew up around here somewhere and although the bank robbed was not in Deadwood, the crime occurred in this District. Matt needed to refresh his recollection so he walked down the street and into the office of the Black Hills Weekly News. He saw one of the publishers, Bill Miller, at his desk.

"Bill, about three or so years ago we had this trial in town of a tall, red headed kid who robbed a bank near here somewhere. I know you keep copies of old newspapers. Would you have a copy of one from that period?"

Bill, who was reputed to have the best memory in South Dakota, thought a minute and said, "You'd be talking about Arron Begley. The robbery occurred in Custer City. I'm sure we have a copy of the paper."

Bill walked into the back room and returned in about five minutes with a newspaper in his hands.

"Can I assume, Matt, that Begley is a suspect in our recent robbery?"

"You probably can, Bill, but I'd rather you not, at least for a while. He doesn't know I know and I like it that way."

Matt stood at the counter and read the article in the old newspaper. Red had grown up on a small ranch just outside Cheyenne Crossing and the bank he robbed was in Custer City, only a few miles south of there. It seemed Red likes to stay close to home. He must have just gotten out of prison when he struck Deadwood, ten miles north of Cheyenne Crossing. The family ranch, if they still own it, might make a good hideout.

Matt knew there wasn't much in Cheyenne Crossing, a few small ranches and a way- station built to service the Cheyenne to Deadwood stage. The stage stopped there long enough to change horses and for the passengers to relax and have a hot meal. The men might stand around the bar and smoke a cigar and enjoy a drink. The station, open to all who might wish to come that far, has a reputation for excellent food and liquor.

Matt expressed his thanks to Will Miller and walked back to his office. Matt sat at his desk and summed up what he knew and what he could reasonably deduce. First, Red Begley, and his three remaining gang members, remain in the area. He knows this because their hideout is close enough to send a gang member into Deadwood in order to check on the health of those Red shot. The old Begley ranch, just outside Cheyenne Crossing, is only ten miles away.

The newspaper had reported that Red's mother was dead at the time of his trial and that his father who was in very bad health attended the trial but seemed greatly embarrassed by the act of his son. Matt guessed that the father had died during Red's time in prison or Red would not go home. With the father gone, if Matt's guess was right, the ranch would not be well stocked and the gang might be having their meals at the station house. It was worth a ten-mile trip to find out.

***

Matt gathered a posse of six men and thy arrived at the Cheyenne Crossing way-station at ten the following morning. They were in time for breakfast and took advantage of it. A man who appeared to be in charge walked over to Matt.

"I see from your badge you're a marshal. From Deadwood?"

"Deputy, actually. Yes we are from Deadwood. Have you seen a tall, redheaded man in here lately?"

"I suppose you're referring to Red Begley. Everyone knows 'wild Red.' He was in here last night with some friends. Is Red in trouble again?"

"Perhaps. Would you know where his family ranch is?"

"I do. There's a crossroad just a little further up. Turn left and the ranch is about two miles on your left. You can't miss it. His father died about a year ago and the place is already grown up."

Matt and the posse members finished their breakfast and headed for the ranch. As indicated, it wasn't hard to find. Four horses were saddled and tied in front of the house as if the occupants might soon move on. Matt sent two members of the posse to cover the rear of the house with rifles, one was sent to each side of the house and two were placed in strategic spots in front. Matt then walked quietly up to the horses tied in front of the house, untied them from the rail and, after walking them away from the house, tied them to a fence further up the road. Then from behind a tree, he shouted, "Red, you're wanted outside."

After some delay, Matt heard a voice, "Who wants me?"

"I'm Matt Harding, the deputy sheriff of Deadwood. I want you for robbin' our bank and shootin' two men. Your house is surrounded by men with rifles so it'd be better if you just came out."

"What'd you do with our horses?"

"They're available if you come out with your hands up. But they won't be available if you come out shootin' and you won't need them if you make us blast you out."

Red sent one of his men to open the back door and look around. As the door opened, a bullet struck it high up.

"Red, I forgot to tell you. If you want to come out with your hands up, it must be through the front door."

Matt heard whispering inside the house. Finally four men walked out with their hands up.

They were taken back to Deadwood and placed in a cell well away from Roy.

A few days later when they appeared in court with lawyers, the identification of Red by Sid White was sufficient to hold him without bail. Matt had to agree that the only evidence against the others was guilt by association. The Judge wouldn't buy it and they were released on bail. At this same appearance before the Court, Roy pled guilty to attempted robbery, a lesser crime the prosecutor believed justified because of Roy's attempt to help Sid, and was sentenced to three years in the federal correction facility located near Custer City.

***

It was now two weeks after the arrest of Red Begley and the town was awaiting his trail in two weeks. Red's lawyer wanted a speedy trial because Sid's condition had worsened and it did not appear he could testify.. The sheriff was back from a successful hunting vacation and Matt was enjoying again merely being "deputy."

The following morning, Matt was called in to see the sheriff.

"Matt, I saw Hector Shaw who's prosecuting Begley and he said there's a meeting in Judge Watson's office at four o'clock. In addition to the judge and Hector, Clyde Barton, Begley's lawyer, will also be there. Shaw has asked that you also attend. My guess is it has to do with Sid White's death. It appears Shaw is without his material witness."

When Matt arrived, the meeting was in progress. The Judge motioned Matt to have a seat.

"We appreciate you coming, Deputy. Let me fill you in on what's going on. You must know by now that Sid White died last evening caused by from complications his having been shot during the robbery. Mr. White had identified Clyde's client as the shooter but because he will not be subject to cross-examination the statement is hearsay and will not be admissible. Understandably, Clyde has moved to have the charges dismissed and his client released because the State won't be able to prove its case without the testimony of Mr. White."

"What can I do, Judge?"

"I'll get to that. There is, of course, another potential witness, the young robber shot during the robbery."

"He refused to identify anyone, Judge."

"Hector, you take it from here."

"Matt, I thought perhaps the reason Roy Acres refused to name names and testify against Mr. Begley is because we had a better witness, a respected member of the community. I hope that if he knows the bank customer shot by Begley . . . "

"Allegedly shot by Begley," interposed Begley's lawyer.

. . . Mr. Acres might be willing to testify in order to keep the man who allegedly shot him from going free. I've been at the telegraph office most of the day conversing with the warden of the facility where Acres is being held. I told the warden to advise Acres that if he will cooperate and testify, I'll recommend the territorial governor commute his sentence. The short of it is that Acres is willing to testify without the commutation of his sentence. He fears, however, that an effort will be made to kill him before he gets to Deadwood. His condition for testifying is that you personally pick him up from the prison."

"Will they permit that?"

"The warden says he will turn Acres over to you is you have a court order granting you custody. I have asked the Judge for such an order."

"Do you have any objections, Clyde?" asked the Judge.

"Only that it might not be good for my client."

"That's insufficient. I'll grant the Order. Now, Deputy, how do you plan to get Mr. Acre here and get him before the scheduled trial?"

"Obviously, Judge, I haven't had time to plan the move in detail but I suppose I'll bring him on the Cheyenne-Deadwood stage by getting' on at Custer City. I believe I can get prison guards to bring him the short distance to Custer City."

"Will that not put the other passengers at risk?"

"I will try not to do that. I'll go talk to the local manager of the stage line about arrangin' for a specially scheduled stage with guards as the only passengers. If I can't do that, I'll take a posse of a few men and we'll bring him back by horse. Because the opposition only has to kill the witness and not take him from my custody, both my plans have risks. If I use the stage, even if it is well-fortified, they can lay an ambush and, if they are close enough, shoot into the stage windows.

"I can reduce this risk by stopping the stage when an obvious ambush site appears near and sending a rider to check it out. I will keep my horse with me.

"Basically the risk will remain but if we take horses at least we can check obvious places of danger which will not have to be close. They will know what Roy looks like and from over two hundred yards a good marksman can pick him off.

"In any event, I have a while to refine my plan."

***

Matt saw Glen Hill, the local manager of the Black Hills Stage and Express Line, sitting on the walkway outside his office.

"Good morning, Glen. Great day."

"It is that, Matt. But you know with the demise of Sam Bass and his gang, every morning is great. Did you know Bass robbed our stage four times during a two-month period in 1877? Is this a business trip or social?"

"Both but primarily business mostly. I need to bring an inmate from the prison near Custer City here for Red Begley's trial. Begley's gang might try to stop me. Obviously I don't want to put any passengers at risk so I need the entire stage. What can you do?"

"Probably a lot. Our management hates all thieves, whether they rob banks or holdup stages. We believe that one who robs a bank is just as inclined to holdup a stage. Robbers see a stage as merely a horse-drawn bank."

"Here's what I'll recommend to my bosses. We have an ironclad coach called the 'Monitor' that we used when gold shipments were so often targeted. We haven't used it for some time but it's in storage and in good condition. I know they'll insist on using our driver which Deadwood will have to pay and you'll have to provide your own security."

"There'll be no charge for the coach. Will that help?"

"It sounds great, Glen. How long before you know?"

"I pretty well know now but I'll confirm it within the hour. When do you need it?"

"The next two or three days would be good."

"I'll get right on it."

Within an hour, Glen came to the sheriff's office with confirmation. "The ironclad will be at the Custer City stage office on Friday morning."

The next morning, Thursday, Matt rode up to Custer City to oversee the preparation for the trip. Four guards with five shotguns would meet him at the stage office in Custer City Friday morning. He would use the fifth shotgun. After he had examined the coach and decided on the seating arrangements, he checked the local newspaper, the Custer City Weekly Chronicle. He often did this when he was out of town to see what was going on around him.

He noticed they had a reporter, Art Webster, young and clearly ambitious. He was similar to a reporter in Deadwood who went out of his way to provoke politicians. If he couldn't find fire, he'd report on smoke. It made him unpopular but substantially increased circulation. Matt would like to talk to him. He also had other arrangements he had to make.

Then he would have dinner and await tomorrow's adventure.

***

The next morning Matt arrived at the Black Hills Stage and Express Line, Custer City branch, around nine o'clock. The Cheyenne stage to Deadwood had arrived and the passengers were getting a short break for breakfast while the horses were being changed. Matt's iron-clad coach sat a few feet away and his driver and guards were having coffee inside the station. His prize passenger had not yet arrived.

Matt remained carefully observant. There were several possible places where the gang might make their move. Here, with the confusion of the two stages, was one.

They started boarding the Cheyenne stage. Matt watched as an old, gray-haired, gray- bearded man had to be helped aboard by a much younger companion, perhaps grandson. The old man was physically picked up and lifted through the door and then helped to his seat beside a woman no longer young but still agile enough to enter the stage unattended. It convinced Matt that stagecoaches were not designed for the elderly.

Just as the stage was filled, a middle-aged man in minister garb rushed to the station master, "Is there room for me on that stage?"

"No as you can see it's filled."

"How about this odd-looking stage. Where's it going?"

"It's also going to Deadwood but it's hired by the deputy over there and I have no control over it."

The man rushed to Matt. "Do you have any room on this stage?"

Matt wondered if this was a coincidence or not. Could the man deliberately have gotten here late in an effort to get on Matt's stage? If so, Matt would rather have him on board where he can be carefully watched rather than following looking for an opportunity.

"Why do you have to get to Deadwood in such a hurry?"

"My sister is getting married tomorrow night and although I'm not officiating, I'd love to be there."

"Reverend . . .?"

"Smythe, Abernathy, an Episcopal minister."

"Yes, Reverend. We have room for one more but I must warn you I'm taking a prisoner back to Deadwood and some people may want tostop me. It could be dangerous."

"Deputy, I know you'll have adequate guards and with an armored coach, I feel perfectly safe."

"I must take some precautions. Open you coat."

The reverend did. "No pistol," he said.

"Raise your pant legs."

He did. "No ankle holster," he said.

"Open your valise."

He did. "No weapons of any kind."

Finally, as an apparent afterthought, "open the Bible you have in your hand."

"Deputy, you are careful." He opened the Bible, "It has not been hollowed out for a pocket pistol."

"Go ahead and have a seat in the stage. You'll be sitting between two shotgun guards.

"We'll be leaving as soon as my special passenger gets here."

It was an hour later when two official looking men walked up with a young man in handcuffs.

"Take the handcuffs off please. He's won't go anywhere."

Matt looked at the new arrival, "Roy, you'll sit across from Reverend Abernathy.

The driver and the outside guard mounted the stage and three inside guards, each with shotguns, entered the stage and sat next to three of the windows. Matt, also with a shotgun, was at the remaining window.

They pulled out of the station about two hours after the regularly scheduled stage. When would the gang strike, Matt wondered.

***

Things were quiet in the stage but you would not expect armed guards responsible for the safety of the passengers to chat away. Finally the reverend, after looking carefully at Roy and the young armed guard next to him, stated, "You know, you two are almost interchangeable. About the same age, the same size, even the same coloring."

"Yeah," said Phil, the young shotgun guard, "but I'm better with a shotgun."

"I'm sure he is," said the young man beside him.

Matt rubbed his chin and thought how observant the good reverend was. I wonder if he believes the similarity in the two young men was purely coincidental.

A couple of miles further up, the stage came to a stop. Matt heard the driver yell, "Deputy, you wanted me to point out any possible ambush spots. We were robbed twice within the last six months in that stand of trees just ahead. You can see where the outcropping of rocks can easily hide someone."

Matt left the stage and, with his shotgun in hand, mounted his horse. After telling the guards to be extra diligent, he first rode around the ambush site and then rode back through it. He stayed there as he signaled the driver to come forward. He tied his horse to the coach and again entered.

There were three more such stops before they pulled up at the Cheyenne Crossing Station.

"All out. We'll be spending the night here. You'll see the food here is outstanding."

The reverend spoke up, "Deputy, I didn't think stage lines had overnight accommodations. Besides, I need to be at the wedding tomorrow."

"Getting to Deadwood tomorrow won't be a problem. We not only have this stage but also the normal Deadwood stage will come through tomorrow about noon. You're right about overnight accommodations, there's normally none. That's one reason for the special stage. I will not risk traveling with my passenger in the dark. Our shotguns would be rendered worthless. I've made arrangements for Roy and me to stay in the manager's quarters and the rest of you can sleep in chairs. We'll leave in the morning at first light."

The reverend made no fuss about the decision, not that it would have done him any good. More likely, however, it is because this decision was anticipated. Clearly trying to deliver a witness at night when someone wanted to stop you would be hazardous.

After the evening meal, the reverend said he was ready for sleep and intentionally sat in an isolated section of the station. The others were unable to see him when he unlocked the side door of the station about an hour before sun up. He opened the door and saw Henry and his two companions coming toward him, He left the door open and quickly entered the big room where he expected the guards to be. No one was there; no one except Roy.

When Henry came in, the reverend stated, "I can't understand where the guards are but there's your man."

"Where?" asked Henry. "That ain't Roy."

"Who in hell are you?" the reverend asked the young man.

"With that language, I might ask you the same thing. My name is Art Webster, a reporter for the Custer City Weekly Chronicle. Because Red Begley's first bank robbery was in Custer City, my editor thought we should cover his upcoming trial. Everyone knew about the special stage so I asked the marshal if I could accompany him. His only condition was that I answer to the name 'Roy' and sit next to him."

"But you were brought to the stage by prison officials."

"They weren't from the prison, they were local lawmen that the deputy provided."

"Then I guess Phil is you, I mean Roy."

"I guess he could be. No one ever said."

"It doesn't matter," said the reverend, "The deputy and his witness are in the station manager's quarters. Since I don't see the shotgun guards, they may be in there with them. "

"No one is in there except the station manager. He went in after everyone left," said the reporter. "The coach returned to Custer City about midnight and the guards, hired there, returned with the coach. I heard the deputy ride out going to Deadwood a few minutes later. Perhaps Roy was with him. I don't like horses so I'm taking today's stage."

Henry addresses one of his companions, "Horace, check the manager's quarters to make sure no one's in there."

Finding only an irate station manager, Horace returned. "What do we do with the reporter, kill him?"

"Horace, you're getting as bad as the boss. How would that benefit us? The newspaper would post a reward and hound us until we're caught. We leave him be. Let's go."

***

Matt slept in late and went to the marshal's office mid-morning. As he walked in, he saw the old man with the gray hair and beard sitting next to the young man who helped him onto the stage in Custer City. That young man was now wearing a deputy's badge.

"Well, Troy, I see you and Roy made it alright."

"You had a good plan, Matt. We had no trouble at all."

"Maybe he didn't but I found the trip very unenjoyable. He wouldn't let me talk at all."

"Matt, you weren't able to disguise his voice. He sounds like a teenager."

"When can I remove the whiskers?"

"Roy, I'd like you to remain disguised for a while. Red has had a regular visitor and we believe he's one of your old gang. Since he's been tryin' to kill you, I suppose you don't mind identifyin' him now."

"No I don't. He doesn't deserve my protection anymore."

It was an hour or so later when a man rushed into the jail. He removed his gun belt as was required of any visitor, placed it on a hook, and advised he wished to visit Begley. Matt looked at Roy who nodded yes and whispered "Henry."

Matt walked over to the visitor and said, "Henry, today we'll let you visit him inside his cell. You're under arrest for being involved in the bank robbery in which Sid White was killed."

"You told the judge earlier you had no witness that I was even at the bank."

"We do now," Matt responded pointing at Roy who haf removed his wig and beard.

"Henry, I wasn't going to rat on you until you set out trying to kill me."

53

"Roy, it wasn't personal. The boss ordered it."

After Henry was led to the cell, Matt suggested he and Roy walk around outside. He reasoned that the other gang members probably came into town with Henry and were waiting for him somewhere nearby. Waiting across the street in front of the saloon were three men. Roy pointed out Horace Abbot and Lee Dexter as the other members of the gang but added, "I don't recognize the other one."

"That's Reverend Abernathy without his clerical duds. I'm not sure what we can charge him with but I'll take all of them into custody."

After their trial, Henry, Horace and Lee were all convicted of bank robbery and were sentenced to ten years in prison. Red was convicted of robbery and murder and sentenced to hang. The reverend pleaded to conspiracy to commit murder and was sentenced to five years. All in all, a satisfactory result.

Roy approached Matt after the verdicts were read and asked how the deputy intended to get him back to prison.

"I tell you, Roy, if you want to go back to prison you'll have to arrange your own transportation. The prosecutor asked the governor to commute your sentence even if you didn't want him to. The Governor did and you're a free man."

"Damn, Deputy, what'll I do now," said Roy smiling, "I'm a terrible bank robber and I hate ranching. I guess I'll try acting with Buffalo Bill Cody's traveling wild west show.

POST SCRIPT. During this period there was a Cheyenne to Deadwood stage that went through Custer City and Cheyenne Crossing. Sam Bass did hold up the stage four times within two months. Bass was later shot in an ambush in Round Rock, Texas by Texas Rangers and died from wounds received in that encounter.

An ironclad coach, called the Monitor, was owned by the stage line and it was also held up by outlaws. The company had an additional armored stage known as "Old Ironsides" which ran on its Deadwood – Sidney route. It was also held up.

The Custer City Daily Chronicle did exist for a while as did the Deadwood paper.

Attacking the Deadwood stage was a regular feature in Cody's wild west show.

AMENDS

After three years, Kerk Holden has finally been released from the Union army. It was now late summer in the year 1868, over two years since the end of the war. He rode his horse in the newly created Wyoming Territory slowly and without a specific destination. He had been released from the army at Fort Laramie and was now riding southerly, generally in the direction of Laramie City some miles away. He's seeking something but just what eludes him.

He's not searching for himself as much as searching for a place where he can be himself, or rather a better self. He's not proud of some of his past and since he can't change it, he'd like to make amends for it. That would be sort of changing it or at least mitigating it. It's his life starting now for which he wants to be remembered. Laramie could be a "start-over" town.

Kerk's mother died in childbirth and his father raised him on a ranch in Oklahoma until his father' death. Kerk was fifteen. Rather than live with his uncle and stay in Oklahoma, Kerk left the family ranch in charge of his uncle who promised to care for it for him. He then moved to Texas to make his own way. He worked on a ranch for a couple of years before he met the Owens brothers in a saloon in Dallas. They took a liking to him and offered him a job at their livery. Kerk took the job.

Both Owens brothers were good with a gun, especially Jim. They would often set up targets at the livery and practice their draw and their shooting. They would invite some of the local youths, including Kerk, to participate. They taught Kerk extremely well. So well that Jim Owens called him aside one day and said to him, "Junior, I have seen very few people as fast as you. Remember that having a fast gun is no reason to kill; it's only a means to protect yerself. Me and my brother are both fast and yet we never shot anyone."

After teaching him to shoot straight and draw fast, they taught him how to rob banks. In order to supplement their income, the Owens would occasionally hit banks in small towns some distance from Dallas. They chose small banks even though the money would be less because it would reduce the risk that shooting would be required. They ordinarily took Bill Rooter, an older man who also worked at the livery, with them on their robberies to hold their horses in order to assure they'd be immediately available when they left the bank. They decided to replace Rooter because his physical condition was making their getaway more problematic. They asked Kerk to take his place. Jim told him the risk would be small and the profits large. Their action would, of course, be illegal. It seemed exciting and Kerk said yes.

Kerk participated in three robberies before they journeyed to a small town in north Texas. Here the authorities were waiting for them. The Rangers had set an ambush. The Owens brothers followed their normal routine with the brothers entering the bank and having their horses held ready when they came running out. Because the banks would not accommodate robbers by having a horse rail right outside the bank, the horses were held a short distance from the bank ready when the brothers exited. Kerk, now eighteen, was assigned to hold the horses.

The Rangers had been warned the Owens were coming. They were inside the bank pretending to be tellers and customers. Kerk always thought Bill Rooter had sold the Owens' out for replacing him. Kerk was grateful that Rooter only knew him as Junior.

The brothers had no chance. As soon as they entered the bank, the shooting started. Kerk saw Roy Owens stagger out of the bank and fall to the boardwalk. When Jim didn't immediately come out, Kerk knew they had him trapped inside the bank. Kerk dropped the reins of the other two horses and rode quietly out of town. He knew the Rangers would soon be on his trail so when he hit a grassy area just out of sight of the bank where his track would be less visible, he jumped from his horse and drove it away in a southerly direction believing the Rangers would follow the horse. He then slipped back into town and went into a saloon to wait it out. There were only three men in the saloon when he entered and they paid no attention to him as he ordered a whiskey. The men talked about having heard gunfire but it wasn't important enough for them to leave their drinks.

In a few minutes, a man ran into the saloon proclaiming that the Rangers had killed two men in a bank robbery. "The lead ranger is very upset that one may have gotten away. They found two horses up the street from the bank that they believe were owned by the robbers. What upsets him though is they found other tracks they believe may belong to a third member of the gang. The Rangers are now out tracking the third horseman who headed south from town."

Kerk finished his drink and walked out of the saloon. He walked up the street to another saloon with eight horses tied to the rail. He untied the reins of what appeared to be the best horse, mounted it, and rode out of town going north. No one spotted him. He rode into Oklahoma and kept going. After several days, he entered the Wyoming Territory and enlisted in the army.

At first, the army had been his sanctuary. Then it became his home. He came to deeply regret his time with the Owens brothers. He promised himself that someday he would set things right.

The last sign he saw indicated Laramie was five miles away. He headed that way. His canteen had been empty for some time and he was thirsty. He decided to stop at the next ranch and ask to fill his canteen. A ranch house about a hundred yards off the road came into view and he headed for it. As he approached, he heard voices.

"Ya sign the deed, Foster, or ya'll die."

"Then you'll have to kill me, Chester."

"What about your daughter standin' beside you? She'll also haf to die. She'll be accidently killed in our gunfight."

"There's not going to be a gunfight. All I have is a rifle and it's in the house."

"Now ya have a revolver," said Chester tossing a handgun at Foster's feet.

Kerk rode up to the group and dismounted.

"And who 'er ya?" asked Chester.

"I'm just a friend of Foster's. Why don't I substitute for him in this gunfight you're so keen to have?" Kerk squared himself and faced Chester. "I'm ready when you are."

Chester stared at Kerk. "You seem to think yer good with a gun."

"Oh, I am."

"Killed a lot of men?"

"I've never come in second. Since you are still alive, you must also have avoided a second-place finish. This should be an interesting gunfight."

"Not today. Ya're too sure of yerself. I'll get ya later, perhaps you won't be lookin'."

Chester mounted his horse and prepared to ride away.

"You know, Chester, if you'd made that threat to me in Texas a few years ago, I'd have shot you down in order to avoid being shot in the back later. But I've learned that a coward who picks only on those he believes are weaker than himself is not really a threat, especially to one who can and will kill him with the least provocation. Now go on and slink away."

Chester said nothing as he rode off.

"Mr. Foster, I stopped to see if I can fill my canteen."

"Certainly, let my daughter, Abby, fill it for you." Abby took the canteen and entered the house.

"And what is the name of the man who came to my rescue?"

"Newkerk Holden. People call me Kerk, spelled with an 'e.' Newkerk is my uncle's name."

"I didn't think I'd ever be beholden to a gunfighter but I am."

Abby returned with his canteen.

Kerk picked up the gun Chester had thrown to Foster and examined it. "Funny thing about this gun, it has no bullets.

"I should probably set things straight. I'm not a gunfighter or at least I've never been in a gunfight. I didn't lie to Chester although I misled him. I am very good with a gun and that's a fact. During my training, this was before I went in the army and while I was still in Texas, we would have competitions but since we didn't want to kill our friends, we would set up targets and have someone judge the quickness of our draw. I wasn't just a little better I was by far the best both in speed and accuracy. My reputation spread within the community and the locals would never challenge me. In fact, I have never been challenged. I can therefore honestly say I've never come in second in a gunfight."

Abby asked, "Where are you heading?"

"Nowhere in particular. The army just released me and I'm looking for a place to settle down, at least for a while. I thought Laramie might be a place I can find a ranch job."

"If a job is what you want, why don't you work for me?" asked Foster. "Abby is a beautiful young woman but she's not a great ranch hand. I'll provide you room and board and what's normally paid around here. You'll find that Abby is a great cook."

"I'll take it. Where's the bunkhouse?"

The bunkhouse in my upstairs bedroom."

***

Early the next morning, Abby called Kerk down to breakfast. Abby proved to be a good cook and, as her father said, a beautiful young woman. Kerk judged her to be about twenty, five feet six and a hundred twenty pounds. She had black hair, clear skin and a nice figure. All in all, he liked his new employers.

After breakfast, they hitched the wagon and headed the five miles into Laramie for supplies.

After they loaded their supplies, Abby wanted to stop at a dry goods store to obtain material for a new dress. Foster and Kerk waited in the wagon outside the store. Kerk noticed that Chester, now wearing a badge, was talking with a young man dressed in black with his holster belted low. The earmarks of a gunfighter, thought Kerk.

Kerk also noticed a big man, also with a badge, standing a few feet away from Chester.

Foster whispered to Kerk, "The big man is deputy marshal "Big Steve" Long. Some say you can hardly distinguish him from the outlaws. He and his brothers who run the family saloon have a habit of coming into ownership of ranches whose owners sign over their property to them and then immediately leave town. It is said that many who refused to sign over their land or mining claims were later found dead. There's never been a witness who came forward."

"That seems very similar to what Chester tried to do to you yesterday. Is Chester Long's deputy?"

"It would seem that way except the office is not actually run by Long. Long's half-brothers formed Laramie City with Ace Moyer, Long's half-brother, becoming Justice of the Peace and Con Moyer. his other half-brother, became marshal. Last year, Con named "Big Steve" as his deputy."

The man dressed in black was walking toward them when a young woman, a blond young woman, grabbed his arm. Kerk couldn't hear what was said between them but he saw the man shake off her hand and proceed in his direction.

Foster said, "That's Bert Williams; he now fancies himself a gunfighter. Abby used to be in love with him. Before Bert's father died, they lived on a ranch next to us. The kids always played together. After his father's death, the mother sold the ranch and moved into town. Bert was a good kid then. Bert's sister, Alice, just tried to stop him from coming over. She knows what he is up to. I'm afraid you're about to be challenged."

"It had to happen.

Bert walked over to wagon.

"You insulted my friend, Chester, by calling him a coward and that's an insult to me. Get down off the wagon and face me."

"You seem proud to call a coward a friend. That doesn't speak very highly of you. I see why you're insulted.

"Marshal Long, do you have any problem with our resolving this matter in this way?"

"You're adults. Do what you want."

Kerk stepped down from the wagon and moved far enough to get Foster out of the line of fire. "And what's the name of the person I'm about to kill?" he asked.

"I guess you ought to know who's about to leave you in the dirt. My name is Bert Williams."

"Why are you doing this, Bert?"

"I told you. Chester is my friend."

"And you think that defending a cowardly friend is a good enough reason to die. Do you have any last words?"

"Yeah, you're a dead man."

With that, Bert drew his gun but the barrel had not cleared his holster when he felt a bullet tear through his shoulder knocking him to the ground and causing his gun to fly a few feet away. Kerk walked over to him and kicked the gun even further away. Bert's sister came running up and knelt beside Bert. She looked at Kerk, "You shot him."

"Yes."

"You could have killed him."

"Yes."

"Why didn't you?"

"At the last second, I decided it wasn't necessary."

"Thank you." She stood and followed the men carrying Bert toward the doctor's office

Chester walked up, "You make it sound like you intentionally didn't kill him. The fact is that you're fast as lightening but you can't hit anythin'."

"Chester, you'll have to take my word that I hit what I shoot at. If you want, I'll prove it now."

Marshal Long separated them saying there had been enough excitement for the day and Kerk rejoined the Fosters at their wagon.

They were about to return to the ranch when Alice Williams walked up. The girls warmly greeted each other.

"Alice, will Bert be alright?"

"Thanks to your friend, he'll be fine, Abby. At least, that's what the doctor thinks."

Foster looked at Kerk, "Wasn't it dangerous for you to just shoot him in the shoulder?"

"Not too dangerous. He was so slow I had ample time to try to disarm him and still have time for a second shot if he held on to his gun. He's lucky he is not a real gunfighter."

"Well, I guess we're lucky it wasn't Long himself who challenged you," said Foster.

"I'm not sure," said Kerk, "and I'm not being immodest."

"How can you say that, Kerk? You haven't seen Long draw."

"No, but he saw me. He must consider me an embarrassment with my calling his deputy a coward and this would have been a good time to challenge me if he thought he was much faster. You must consider he would have to believe himself noticeably faster, not just as fast. Instead he just walked away."

Abby asked, "Why noticeably faster?"

"There's nothing worse than two men with the same ability drawing on each other. You'd have to bury two men."

***

A few days later, Mr. Foster and Kerk had just returned from taking thirty head of cattle to market in Cheyenne and were enjoying a drink when Abby announced that she had invited Bert, Alice and their mother to Sunday dinner. They accepted. She explained that she had enjoyed seeing Alice in town so much that she wanted to rekindle the friendship between their families.

Foster looked at his daughter, "I think I know whose friendship you want to rekindle. Kerk, I hope you won't be embarrassed by having Bert sitting at the dinner table."

"Why should I? After all, he has the sore shoulder." He paused, "I apologize for that. Abby, I know you will enjoy seeing Bert so much that I can't possibly have any objection."

"Well, I noticed the way you looked at Alice and I believe you'll be just as happy to see her. And, Dad, it won't hurt for you to have dinner with an attractive woman either. It's been three years since mother died."

"Sally is an attractive woman but please leave me out of any match making."

Sunday came and there was initially a little tenseness when Bert walked into the house with his arm in a sling. He took care of that immediately.

"Kerk, I apologize for challenging you the other day. It was stupid in more than one way. First, of course, you are much faster. Second, and I think this need be said for the sake of Abby and my mother, and not as an excuse but as an explanation. I always planned to be a rancher. I enjoyed ranching and I always assumed I'd take over our ranch when Dad died. I never thought what would happen if Dad died before Mom. I understand her not wanting to stay on the ranch after Dad's death. Selling the ranch was necessary to support her in town.

"The problem is that this left me twenty years old with no plans and no future. That's why I stopped coming around to see Abby. I had nothing to offer her. That hurt me more than anything else. So I started looking around town for some kind of work that would be acceptable.

Think about it. What kind of work can a former ranch hand do? The town is divided into two groups: those who like Deputy Long and those who despise him. The ones who like him seem to be doing much better. That's why I befriended Chester, to get in good with Long. It worked. Long took an interest in me. He even taught me how to draw and to shoot, obviously not good enough. I now realize how stupid it was for me to be willing to kill someone for a worthless person like Chester. Kerk, I'm sorry."

Kerk hesitated trying to decide how much to say.

"Bert, I've made bad decisions in my past. I won't discuss the facts now but I decided, after I got out of the army, I'd make things right. That's why I intervened when Chester challenged Mr. Foster and it's why I only winged you. I still have a lot of making up to do. Perhaps you do too."

"Yes, but you know I can't draw fast like you. What can I do?"

"There are many ways to do good without using a gun. For example, Mr. Foster gave me a job even though he and Abby were well able to handle this operation. I accepted it because I thought Chester might return. And by accepting responsibility for a bad decision and by wanting to go in a different direction, you have made a very good start."

Sally Williams spoke up. "Bert, I had no idea you wanted to ranch that land. You never mentioned it. I could see you leaving home soon and I'd be there all alone. I'm sorry.

"Paul, the man who bought the ranch from me approached me last month saying he wished to reduce his operation and asked if I'd be willing to buy back fifty acres. I told him no but I imagine the offer would still be good. That would be a good start for Bert. If I bought the fifty acres and put fifty head of cattle on it, would you help him get started?"

"Certainly, I would. After selling off some cattle this week, I probably have about a hundred head remaining. He could run his fifty head with my herd and we'd split the profits two thirds, one third. That is if my partner agrees. What do you say, Abby?"

"I can't think of a better plan, Dad."

Foster looked at Kerk, "What would you think of working with Bert?"

"Mr. Foster, I thank you for asking. But that would add an additional burden to all of you. I never thought this would be a permanent job. I'll stay until Bert's arm is well enough for him to be back in working shape and then I'll move on."

After lunch, Abby and Bert walked off together and Foster and Sally Williams went into the parlor to discuss the cattle merger further. Kerk walked out to the porch to give them privacy. He was soon joined by Alice.

"Kerk, suppose no one wants you to leave?"

"It only makes sense, Alice."

"Suppose I don't want you to leave?"

"That would certainly make leaving much harder. You've seen how I look at you. I hope to be able to get another job somewhere near Laramie and still be near you. How many young men will I have to fight off?"

Alice walked up to Kerk and put her arms around his neck. "I asked you to stay. That should tell you. I see you as being different from the other men around here and I like the difference."

Kerk pulled her close and kissed her..

"No. Not like that. She pulled his head down hard on hers and kissed him passionately.

"Isn't that better?"

"I've never kissed or been kissed like that. But I'd say it's better. If you did it again, I'd probably know."

Abby and Bert came walking onto the porch. "We thought we'd better join you."

As the guests departed after lunch, everyone agreed to meet again at the rancher's association dance the following Friday in Laramie.

***

Foster, Abby and Kerk arrived at the dance at seven thirty and gathered around the punch bowl. A few minutes later, Sally Williams, Bert and Alice arrived and came over to join them.

Bert, looking angry, said, "My shoulder has been hurting all day."

He then hit Kerk in the face, knocking him to the floor and then fell on top of him.

"Lay still and listen," he whispered to Kerk. "Three men are planning to kill you when you go out the front door. Chester is in the wagon across the street with a rifle, Smiley Green is in the alley in case you go out that way and a third man is in here planning to follow you out. I don't know who it is but you can bet he's watching us now. Chester came by to check on my shoulder today and thought this news would cheer me up. If Long finds out I told you, I'm sure he'll kill me."

Kerk pushed out from under Bert and stood up. He pulled Bert to his feet and pushed him across the room. "If you come anywhere near me again tonight, I'll break your other arm." Kerk walked away from everyone and stood in the corner near the band. Soon he was joined by Foster and the three women.

Mrs. Williams was the first to speak, "Kerk, I'm so sorry. I don't know what came over him."

Kerk whispered to them, "I'm going to tell you something but I don't want your expressions to change and I don't want you to look at Bert. He just saved my life but if Long finds out, he'll likely have Bert killed. Three men plan to kill me when I walk out the front door. Chester is across the street in a wagon with a rifle, someone named Smiley Green is in the alley and a third is in here planning to follow me out. Since I now know the plan, I'm not concerned about my safety but I am worried just how I can handle this without putting Bert at risk.

"Mr. Foster, I looked out the window as I walked over here and saw the wagon. It's hitched to two horses. I assume some rancher came to the dance in the wagon. When you get a chance, see if you know who owns the wagon. If you do, without telling him too much, see if you can get him to go home early. Without Chester and his rifle covering the front door, their plan will fall apart."

Foster and Sally walked to the dance floor and danced around the room to where Foster could get a view across the street. "That's Ed Larson's rig. I see him and June at the refreshment table. Excuse me."

Foster walked over and greeted Ed warmly and asked if Ed would join him for just a minute. They walked to where they could talk privately.

"Ed, I don't want to get into the details too much but we have a problem. Chester is in your wagon with a rifle. You'd be doing all of us a favor if you moved your wagon. If you just called it a night and went home it would be even better. I will explain fully the next time I see you."

"No problem, I'm ready to go anyhow."

Ed walked over to June and took her arm. "Make no protest and follow me." He led her out to their wagon and seemed surprised to see Chester who had just sat up. "Chester, what are you doing in my wagon?"

"I was making my rounds and decided to sit in your wagon and listen to the music. I must have fallen asleep. I'll get out now."

Chester jumped down from the wagon and started walking up the street. He was soon joined by a man who had been standing in the alley.

Foster, who was looking for the inside man, saw Tim Ayres leave when Chester walked away. Not absolute proof but very suspicious. Just to be sure though, they continued to avoid Bert until it was time to leave and Bert, accompanied by his mother and sister, went home.

As Foster, Abby and Kerk headed back to the ranch, Kerk commented, "That's twice since I faced Chester down at your place that he has tried to have me killed, once, by using Bert and again tonight. I told him what would happen if he tried anything. I either have to face Long who's behind it or take care of Chester."

"Hold off a few days," said Foster. "Plans are in the making now that might resolve this problem. There's going to be a meeting of interested citizens to discuss Long tomorrow night.

"I'd like for you to come with me."

***

The meeting was at the home N. K. Boswell, a local rancher who had served as the first sheriff of Albany County. The meeting was about Long and his two half-brothers, Con and Ace Moyer. The brothers and Long owned a saloon referred to by the townspeople as the "Bucket of Blood" because of all the violence that took place in it.

Boswell addressed the group of ranchers and interested townspeople, "You all know about Long. He doesn't mind killing people. As soon as he became deputy marshal he killed five men who were engaged in a street brawl. Some might consider that excessive.

There is some evidence that he extorted several ranchers out of their land on the threat of death and killed others, in self-defense he claims, who had not given over their land to him and his brothers. I told you at our last meeting that if we watched Long closely enough we'd catch him committing a crime and we could take action with the law on our side. That time has come.

"Recently, Long attempted to rob a prospector, Rollie "Hard Luck" Harrison. A gun fight ensued with Long wounded and Harrison killed. Although Harrison died before he could name his assailant, Long told his fiancée what had occurred. She was so upset she came to me. I got a statement from her and then called this meeting. Tomorrow we'll meet outside the Bucket of Blood and see justice enforced."

That's precisely what happened. The vigilantes went into the saloon and came out with the three brothers, led them to a partially completed cabin and hanged them from the rafters.

A week later there was again a gathereing at Foster's ranch for dinner. Kerk led Alice again to porch for an important question. But before asking Alice to marry him, Kirk told her of his past and asked if she could accept it.

"Well," she said, "on the one hand we have a teenager who made a dumb mistake. However he caused injury to no one. On the other hand we find that same person at some personal risk saved the life of a rancher and his daughter from Chester and then only wounded a man who insisted on a gunfight when anyone else would have killed him. This same man whose life was in danger at the ranchers' dance, found a way to protect the one who had tried to kill him earlier. All in all, I'd say this man's good deeds greatly overshadows Junior's bad deeds and I suggest we never mention Junior again.

"Now I think it's time that we return to our kissing practice. Instead, they were called into dinner.

A double wedding was planned with a third, Paul Foster and Sally Williams, perhaps would not be far behind.

EPILOGUE:

The people and events in this story are, of course, fictional with the following exceptions:

Big Steve Long was the deputy marshal of Laramie City during the time depicted. His half-brothers, Con and Ace Moyer, were involved in the establishment of Laramie City, one becoming justice of the peace and the other mayor and all three brothers were suspected of many criminal activities including requiring ranchers to deed over their land on threat of death. N. K. Boswell, a former marshal, did form the vigilante group that went into the Bucket of Blood and exited with the three brothers on October 28, 1868 and hanged them from the rafters of an incomplete cabin.

No action was ever taken against the vigilantes. Following his death, Long's fiancée erected a marker in his memory.

A BITTER HOMECOMING

Even though Rex Todd grew up with Ezra Boyles in Wichita, Kansas and attended school with him and his brother, Billy Ben, they were never friends. The two brothers, a year's difference in ages and a vast difference in their appearance and intellect, were in the same grade because Billy Ben was held back a year.

The animosity between Rex and Ezra started in the eighth grade when Rex and Ezra were fifteen and Billy Ben was sixteen. Ezra took after his mother and was small, smart and aloof. His father was older than most of the other parents. He owned the local livery as well as a popular saloon. Ezra was a good student and seemed to be preparing to take over the family businesses.

Billy Ben, on the other hand, took after his father. He was big, already six feet tall and weighed close to two hundred pounds. He was neither smart nor handsome and this apparently troubled him so to compensate he became a bully intimidating every boy in school.

Rex, the next largest boy in school, gave up two inches and thirty pounds to Billy Ben and went out of his way to avoid conflict with him. Rex had seen more than once how Billy Ben dealt with smaller boys who showed the courage to stand up to him. He would rush them and take them to the ground and then sit on them, punching them until they cried, "Enough." One morning as several students milled around in front of the schoolhouse waiting for the bell to sound, Billy Ben chose Rex as his next victim. When insults would not provoke Rex,

Billy Ben pushed his sister, Ellie, causing her to fall. This was too much even for a reticent Rex. He pushed Billy Ben back, dropped his book bag to the ground, and waited for the explosion.

"You all saw it," said Billy Ben to the group of onlookers. "He pushed me and now he must pay."

Rex considered his options. He could run but that was out of the question. He'd rather be severely beaten than back down. He could stand his ground and wait for the buffalo to charge and take him to the ground. Billy Ben would then sit on him and beat him senseless. This wasn't an attractive option either. He chose a third option, to be aggressive. He would attack first since the ultimate beating, when it came, would be no worse.

When Bill Ben started his charge, Rex rushed toward him and threw a hard right over Billy Ben's outstretched arms and into his face. The force was even greater because the fist and the face were rushing together. The result was that Billy Ben's nose was badly broken, his lips were split, and he was bleeding profusely. Further, he was knocked back on his heels. As Billy Ben reached to tenderly touch his nose to see if it was broken, he left his considerable belly exposed and unprotected. Rex, fearing the battle was not yet over, attacked Billy Ben's exposed midsection, right, left, right. Billy Ben fell to his knees and seemed to be having trouble breathing but was finally able to utter, "Enough, enough." Either the pain from his nose, his lips, or his midsection, or the humiliation of being so badly beaten, or all of these, caused tears to run down Billy Ben's cheeks.

His classmates were not kind. They cheered and someone shouted, "The bully got his."

One of the boys, a previous victim of Billy Ben's, remarked loudly, "Bully Ben is crying like a baby."

"Or like a girl," another boy added. Even the girls laughed.

Finally the bell rang and the students filed into the schoolhouse, all but Billy Ben who continued to lay on the ground in a fetal position. Billy Ben's greatest humiliation was seeing Ezra, looking clearly disgusted with him as though his defeat had disgraced the family, ignore him and silently walk into the schoolhouse.

Later, after the teacher was advised of the confrontation, she went outside to check on Billy Ben but he was not there. He did not return to school that day. Instead, when he was able to get up, he walked home and, wincing from the utter contempt on his brother's face, got his father's shotgun and turned it on himself.

The news of Billy Ben's death caused different reactions among the student onlookers. Many of those who considered Rex a hero for facing and defeating the bully retained that view believing the world was better off without people like Billy Ben. But there were also those who, although initially believing Rex to have been a hero for facing the bully and who had even cheered his victory, now believed that Rex could have and should have stopped after breaking Billy Ben's nose. By continuing the fight until Billy Ben cried, they reasoned, might have made Rex feel good but it unnecessarily brought humiliation to Billy Ben which led to his death.

Still others, the honest ones, recognized that they, the onlookers, were primarily responsible for the tragedy by cheering Billy Ben's defeat and mocking him. They taunted him for his tears and mercilessly left him alone in his humiliation.

Ezra took it the hardest. Instead of going over and kneeling beside his brother to comfort him, he silently followed the others into the schoolhouse. He saw the hurt in Billy Ben's eyes as he walked away. He will always remember that look. There was no doubt in his mind that Rex was responsible for his brother's death and he would pay dearly. Not immediately and perhaps not directly by his hands but there would be a certain and fitting payback. A life for a life.

But until then, Ezra thought of a petty revenge. Everyone knew Rex was sweet on Sissy Brown, daughter of the owner of the general store. Rex would sit with her at lunch every day. It was a relationship that Ezra knew would go nowhere. Sissy grew up in town and would not settle to live on a ranch. When Ezra asked Sissy to sit with him at lunch a few days later, perhaps due to sympathy for the loss of his brother, she accepted.

Rex was disappointed in seeing Sissy with Ezra but his disappointment increased when Sissy told him later that she was surprised to see his cruelty when he wouldn't stop beating Billy Ben. Further, she added, and this was even more hurtful, she knew Rex liked her so he needed to understand that there was no future for them. They were about to graduate from school and would be expected to go out into the world, find jobs and help their parents or plan for their own marriages. They were now, after all, of marriage age and some of their friends were already talking marriage. He should also know, she advised him, that she could not see herself living on a ranch far from her family, her town friends, and the frequent parties that were so much fun.

With sadness, Rex realized he had never been invited to such a party.

He tried to explain to Sissy that a broken nose was not disabling and that he fully expected Billy Ben to continue the fight with even more determination and he feared the outcome. She was not interested in his explanation.

A month later they finished the eighth grade, the only public education provided at the time. Rex devoted himself to ranching with this father in order to learn all he could about operating his own ranch.

It was well he did. His sister married when she was fifteen and then had a child only to see her husband die during a pneumonia epidemic shortly thereafter. She moved back in with the family and it was understood by everyone that the ranch would go to Ellie when something happened to the parents.

When Rex was seventeen, he decided it was time for him to move on and make provisions to one day purchase his own ranch. He needed a job. Because there was an Indian uprising in Montana, the army was seeking recruits. Rex had the skills the army wanted. He could ride well and was deadly with a rifle. He had never shown interest in handguns but that didn't matter to the army. He joined and was soon sent to Montana.

After they finished school, Rex had not seen Sissy. He wasn't sure whether she avoided him or merely that their paths never crossed. Sissy wasn't beautiful, she was of average height, average weight, and average looks. But he had always found her appealing. He loved her smile and her personality. She would take some getting over.

***

It was not long after gold was discovered in the Black Hills. Because the army was unable, some say unwilling, to maintain the terms of the 1866 Treaty of Laramie and keep settlers and miners out of the Black Hills and off Indian sacred lands, a number of Indians including Sitting Bull declared the treaty broken and left the reservation. Rex was sent to Fort Ellis some sixty or so miles north of Virginia City. Fort Ellis, along with Fort Laramie, would take the lead in driving the Indians back to the reservation.

The army was charged not with defeating the Indians, merely returning them to the reservation. In early skirmishes, Rex's actions, even though he was merely a recruit, came to his officers' attention. He would follow orders explicitly but, more importantly to them, he would show initiative when assigned a particular objective and consider the goal, examine the options, and choose the one most likely to succeed. He was recognized for his tactical ability by being promoted to sergeant. When Custer suffered his humiliating defeat at the Big Horn in June, Rex was given a commission and reassigned to Fort Laramie which would take the lead in the army's response.

And the army did respond. Better weapons and more soldiers flooded into Fort Laramie and action was commenced to avenge Custer's massacre and drive the Indians back to the reservation. It was a successful campaign and within a relatively short period the leaders of the tribes which proved so successful at the Big Horn were either captured or killed. The remainder of the Indians was driven back to the reservation and the Indian wars ended.

When his recruitment ended Rex heard from a fellow officer that his family was having trouble selling their ranch near Dodge City because of the lawlessness in the area. Rex was told the sale of the property, sixty acres with good water, would include cattle too young to market during the last drive. This would constitute a beginning herd. The price was right and Rex who had saved considerable money during his ten years in the army, purchased the property sight unseen. He moved to Dodge City at twenty-seven and became a cattle rancher.

Rex felt he had little reason to return to Wichita and rarely did. His parents were now deceased so he had only his sister and her son, Curt, remaining there. His sister was the only person who knew how to reach him. And reach him she did. He received a wire from his sister.

"I need help" is all it said. He left the ranch in charge of his foreman and traveled to Wichita.

***

After an early start and a hard ride, it was late afternoon when Rex rode up to the small trail leading from the roadway back to the family ranch, now owned by his sister. Something struck him as odd. About a hundred yards further up, a man sat idly on his horse just looking around. Because there was nothing around for concealment, the rider could not help but be conspicuous. Further adding to the mystery was the fact that when Rex turned onto the trail to the ranch, the rider abruptly turned and rode back toward Wichita. Bells went off in Rex's head.

Rex was greeted at the ranch house by his highly distraught sister.

"Ellie, what help do you need?"

"They've charged Curt with murder."

"Tell me about it."

"It happened yesterday. Curt came flying back from town saying they'd be here soon to arrest him. He was coming out of the general store when a local troublemaker approached him. He tried to coax Curt into a fight sort of like the time Billy Ben went after you. When Curt continued to refuse to fight, two shots rang out and the troublemaker fell to the ground. Curt, confused and frightened, jumped on his horse and rushed home. As he was leaving, however, he heard someone shout, "Stop him. I saw him grab Willard's gun and shoot him. He has the gun now. Stop him before he can get rid of it."

"About an hour later the marshal came to arrest Curt. The marshal claimed there was an eyewitness who swears he saw Curt grab the gun out of Willard Hopkin's holster and shoot him. The witness said he'd observed them arguing before the shooting started.

"I told him Curt wouldn't do that.

'Miss Ellie,' the marshal assured me, 'I tend to agree with you. I've known Curt now for several years and the idea that he would shoot someone seems farfetched. But Curt says he didn't do it and the eyewitness swears he did. This makes it a jury question. I'm sorry.

"I asked him who the eyewitness was.

"And he said Ezra Boyles."

Rex looked at his sister for what seemed to her to be a long time. Then he said,

"Accusing Curt of this crime was a way to get me back to town. He knew you'd contact me and that I'd come. They probably watched you go into the telegraph office yesterday to send the wire. They had a man stationed a distance up the road to see when I came. They now know I'm here."

"Why would they do that?"

"You'll remember that when Billy Ben killed himself, Ezra blamed me. He swore he'd get even one day. This seems to be the day. I'd guess they'll come late tonight thinking I'll be tired from the ride from Dodge City and take an early bed."

"If he's that vindictive, I feel sorry for Sissy."

"Why Sissy?"

"She married him the year you went off to the army. We didn't see any reason to tell you."

"Water over the dam. Who's working for you now?"

"Just Josh and Lee who worked for Pa. They're in the bunkhouse."

"Decide what you want to save from the house and we'll move it over behind the barn." Ellie had learned early to rely on Rex's judgment and started surveying her belongings.

Rex walked to the bunkhouse and summonsed Josh and Lee. He told them to harness the horses to the wagon and bring it to the house. They loaded the various things Ellie wanted to save and moved then to a spot behind the barn, unhitched the horses, and returned them to the barn.

"What's this all about, Rex?"

"I'm not absolutely certain, Josh, but I believe in an hour or so, when it gets a little darker, some men will ride up and shoot up the house in order to kill me. More likely though, they'll burn down the house hoping to catch me inside. If I'm right, there will be too many of them for us to fight off. I'm sending Ellie away for a time and I suggest the two of you go into the woods for a spell. They may look in the bunkhouse and the barn for me but I would not expect them to burn either. They have no reason to look behind the barn so I think Ellie's things will be safe. We'd better move now."

Lee saddled Ellie's horse and she left for a three-mile ride to a neighbor's house down the road toward Dodge City, the opposite direction from which Rex anticipated the raiders would come. Josh and Lee gathered a few things and went into the woods. Rex blew out the lamps and left the ranch.

Rex rode about half way to Wichita and found a place to wait and watch. Perhaps he was wrong about Ezra's intentions and all this was unnecessary. He wasn't wrong. Soon a gang of nine men passed going in the direction of Ellie's home. Rex rode on to the outskirts of Wichita and stopped to see if he was right to expect a fire. It wasn't long before a glow reflecting the flames of a fast-growing fire appeared at the location of the ranch house.

Rex now headed for Ezra's family home on the other edge of town. He knocked and Sissy opened the door.

"My God, Rex, what are you doing here?"

"Sissy, I'm here to burn down the house. Please collect whatever you can collect in five minutes and move to the barn."

"Why would you do this?"

"Your husband just burned down my sister's house."

"Is Ellie all right?"

Yes, she's safe and I want you safe also so please hurry."

"There's nothing I want from this house. Everything either belongs to Ezra or he bought it for me. I want nothing to do with it."

"I'm sorry I have to do this but it's essential to my plan."

"It's not simply revenge because I married Ezra?"

"No. I didn't know you'd married him until earlier tonight. Besides I have found revenge gets in the way of careful planning. I want Ezra and his army to rush out here while I do what I have to do in town."

"I was hoping it was because of me. Ezra's army consists of eight gunfighters he just hired. I suppose he was planning for your return."

"Actually, he's responsible for it." Rex started pouring the oil from lamps he found around the house and was surprised to see Sissy also pouring oil all around.

"Why are you doing this?"

"Ezra turned out to be a bigger bully than Billy Ben. In school he didn't have the size or guts to show it. But he's bigger now. I. I finally got tired of his abuse and threatened to go to the marshal. He knew I would and he couldn't stand the thought of others knowing he would beat a woman. He agreed to move into a room in his saloon and leave me here. But he threatened to kill me if I tried to leave. Now, it appears, I'll have no choice."

Sissy moved to the barn as Rex lit the fire. He then rode toward town to find a vantage point to watch and wait for Ezra and his gang to pass. It wasn't long.

***

After Ezra and his gang passed, Rex rode into town and directly to the marshal's office. He entered and found the night marshal who had to stay at the jail when a prisoner was there. He recognized the marshal as a former classmate.

"Rex, it's good to see you."

"Maybe not, George, I want you to release my nephew."

"Rex, I can't do that."

"Listen to me carefully George and I'll tell you why you must. You'll recall Billy Ben's suicide and how Ezra blamed me. He told me one day I'd pay with my life for causing Billy Ben's death. Ezra accused Curt of this crime so Ellie would send for me and he could finally get his revenge. He has assembled an army of gunfighters to help him. Tonight, when he thought I'd be asleep, he burned down Ellie's house. She's safe. It was his declaration of war. I have accepted the challenge. War is not a game; you play to win. A few minutes ago I burned down his house."

"My God, Sissy...?"

"She's fine. The point is, however, innocent people may die in this war. Those who help Ezra almost certainly will. Ezra and his gang are now at his house and will soon realize that I am probably here to get my nephew released. They will come here to stop that and if Curt is still here, Ezra will kill him to get at me. If you don't release him, George, I'll have to take him."

George saw the threat was backed up by the look in Rex's eyes and the Henry repeating rifle held loosely in his hands.

"Okay, Rex, but I want you to lock me in the cell in his place. Ezra can be extremely spiteful."

When Curt was released, Rex took him outside, told him where his mother was, and pointed to the deputy's horse. "Ride out there now and stay until I come get you."

Ezra's saloon was almost directly across the street from the jail so Rex tied his horse to a tree behind the jail. He found a place of concealment and waited.

In a few minutes, Rex heard the sound of horses riding hard from the direction of Ezra's house and saw them pull up in front of the jail. Rex heard swearing as the deputy was released from the cell. Ezra demanded to know what happened.

"Rex came in with that Henry pointed at me and demanded I release the boy. I did and he put me in his place."

"Where'd Todd go?"

"I don't know but I heard horses ride away fast."

One of the gang spoke up, "Ezra, he's probably left town for good. He got the boy released."

"Maybe, but I don't think so. He'll know that if he's not here, I'll simply kill his sister. That'll almost make us even. My guess is that he's still in town. In the morning when it's light we'll go to every house in town until we find him. My manager will have closed the saloon by now. Let's wait there."

Rex overheard the conversation and agreed he could not leave Wichita until Ezra was dead for the very reason expressed by him. This means he'll have to reduce the number of the opposing army by attrition. He waited for the gang to settle down and then, from the darkness across from the saloon, yelled, "Your right, Ezra, I'm still in town and I'll be here until your dead."

Ezra signaled for the two men nearest the door to go out after him. They rushed through the saloon door and a shot rang out, the first man through the door fell to the ground while the other rushed back into the saloon. Rex moved up to the alley to the back of the saloon.

''Boss, we can't see him but the little light from the saloon makes us an easy target."

Ezra thought for a minute, "Hogan, go out the back and circle behind him."

The backdoor opened and Hogan slipped through. Another shot from the Henry and Hogan fell.

"Ezra," one man shouted, "he's got us surrounded."

"You fool, one man can't surround us. He just out thought us. We'll wait until sunup and then go find him."

Rex was extremely tired and need a safe place to rest. He thought of the perfect place. He headed for Ezra's barn.

***

As Rex rode up to Ezra's barn, he saw a light shining from within. Then he heard Sissy's voice, "Who's out there?"

"It's Rex. I need to rest, Sissy, I'll go to the bunkhouse."

"No, come in here."

Rex entered the barn and saw Sissy sitting on a horse blanket next to a lamp.

"I thought you'd have moved back to you mother's house after the fire.

"My parents are both dead. I sold the family home as well as the store so there's nowhere for me to return to. The ironic thing is that I may now have more money than Ezra but I still feel like his prisoner."

"With all that money, why didn't you just move away?"

"Where would I go? Besides, I'd have missed seeing you again."

Rex changed the subject. "I thought we used all the lamps in setting the fire."

"We've always kept one out here. Sit, I want to talk to you. I want to apologize for saying you were cruel for continuing the fight with Billy Ben. I think I knew then and I certainly know now what you

Charles M. Harris

meant by fearing the fight wasn't over and that Billy Ben wouldn't stop until he beat you. That's the way Ezra is. He wanted me only to get at you. I wasn't interested in him. I found that I cared more for you than I imagined. When you didn't come around and then went to the army, there was no one else but Ezra. I was of the age when most all of our friends were married. So I married Ezra and almost immediately knew it was a mistake."

"I accept your apology but it is unnecessary and I'm sorry for the way Ezra treated you."

"I know you're sleepy but you've got to listen. I've been rehearsing this. I know now I was wrong in letting you get away. I want to make amends. I want you."

"Look, either Ezra will kill me or I will kill him. If he is out of the way, your problem will be solved and you probably won't want me."

Sissy moved over to Rex, put her arms around him, and kissed him. And when she kissed him again, he participated.

"I won't let you get away again."

"What's changed?"

"I changed. I was a young, foolish and selfish girl then. Now I'm approaching thirty years old and I'm a sadder but wiser woman."

"But I'm still a rancher and you said you didn't want a rancher."

"I still don't want a rancher, I want you. If that means I have to live on a ranch, so be it. I can see you are about to go to sleep even with me talking. Go ahead. If I hear anything, I'll wake you. But consider what I said."

When Rex awoke, the sun brightly lit the barn. Sissy came running up, "Some horsemen are heading this way. You don't have much time."

Rex saw the horsemen were only a couple of minutes off.

"Tell Ezra I was here but left about an hour ago. Tell him I said I'd given him enough time to sleep and now I was going to town to kill him but that I'd probably come back here."

"Why would you want me to say that?"

"I have a reason."

Rex led his horse around behind the bunk house and waited with the Henry in his hands.

When Ezra dismounted, Sissy approached him.

"Rex was here but he left about an hour ago. He said he'd let you sleep long enough and now he's going to kill you. He also said he'd probably come back here later."

Sissy didn't see the backhand until just before it knocked her to the ground.

"So he spent the night here with you, in the barn of all places."

"Well, we both spent the night in the barn, where else is there?"

Ezra remounted. "Waco," he said talking to a man who had dismounted, "stay her in case he does come back. If he does and you kill him, there'll be a large bonus. If we don't find him in town, we'll be back. Do what you want with the woman. I'll have nothing to do with her after Todd."

With that, Ezra and his remaining troops rushed back to town. Waco looked at Sissy and said, "You know, we can have fun until they come back.

Sissy ran from the barn but after a short chase, she was caught. She was dragged back into the barn.

Rex wanted to delay any shooting until the gang was a little further from them. He picked up a rock and threw it so it landed behind the barn.

Waco whispered to Sissy, "Did ya hear that? Todd's hidin' behind the barn. But you knew that. Now I'll earn that bonus."

As Waco crept quietly toward the back of the barn, Rex entered and stood next to Sissy.

In about three minutes, Waco returned saying, "That was a waste of time. He wasn't there after all."

When Waco reentered the barn with his revolver back in his holster, he faced a determined man with a rifle, "You came back for something. Here it is."

Waco foolishly went for his revolver but he was much too late. Ezra's army was reduced by another man.

Sissy ran up to him with tears in her eyes and hugged him.

"What will you do now? It'll soon be morning and the streets of Wichita will be crowded. You can't go after him now."

"I'll wait here until after the saloon closes tonight and then slip into town and come up behind the saloon. Then I'll see what happens."

"They almost certainly heard the gunfire. Don't you think they'll come back?"

"I doubt it. Ezra has by now probably learned the lesson the Sioux taught Custer: divide your troops at your peril. Custer divided his troops into three and it came back to haunt him. Ezra has now lost a good portion of his army. He should know that if he comes rushing up here, not knowing where I may be hiding along the road, I'll pick off two or more of his men and then disappear. I think he'll wait until I come to town, and he knows I will. The trouble is, what will we do all day?"

Sissy smiled, put her arms around him and said, "I'll think of something. By the way, Ezra tells people he doesn't believe in carrying a gun but you should know he carries a pocket gun, a Derringer I think it's called." She led him back toward the barn.

***

When Rex was some distance from the saloon, he dismounted and led his horse. Then, a little further on, he tied his horse to a tree and quietly approached the rear of the saloon. He stood far enough back so that he could see the entire area behind the saloon. He waited. Then he saw a slight movement just behind the rear door. Ezra had posted a guard here and, almost certainly, in front.

The guard here in the back was sitting on the small deck leading from the rear door. The movement Rex saw was the guard leaning his head back against the wall. The gunmen probably had no sleep for several hours and this one was taking a nap. Rex creeped up beside him and, with the butt of his rifle, extended his nap indefinitely. Rex quietly lowered the guard to the ground and worked his way to the front.

He heard voices from within.

"When we heard the shootin' from your place this mornin' I had hoped that meant Waco had earned his bonus. But even givin' 'em time with the woman, this long delay means you're probably down to five helpers."

"Yeah," replied Ezra, "I thought of that too."

Rex was spotted by the guard in front who went for his revolver. The guard was too late and the sound of the Henry meant Ezra's army was again reduced.

Ezra yelled out, "Clem, did you get him?" No response.

"Harve, check on Otis out back."

Harve inched the door open and saw Otis stretched out on the ground.

"He got Otis too. Ezra, who in hell did you send us up against?"

"I thought eight of you could certainly take care of one man even if he is a war hero.

That's why I hired your whole gang."

Harve paused and then said, "This Todd you wanted us to take care of isn't Captain Todd? His reputation as a smart Indian fighter has spread even to Dodge City. It is said that Captain Todd knew what the Indians were goin' to do before they did. He certainly seems to know what we're goin' to do.

"Ezra, speaking for the three of us remainin', we want more money, a lot more."

"I paid you a lot of money in advance for two weeks of your time. You knew what the job was even if you didn't know who Todd was and you'll get no more money. Now stick to your bargain."

Harve, after making sure the other's agreed, walked to the front entry and shouted out, "Todd, hold yer fire. We've had an employment dispute and we're riding out if you won't shoot us as we leave."

"Come ahead. You have safe passage."

Ezra pleaded, "Wait a minute, Harve. Let's negotiate."

"Ezra, we just don't want to work for you anymore."

The three remaining gunmen walked out of the saloon, mounted their horses and rode out of town.

"I'm coming in, Ezra."

When Rex entered, Ezra was standing under a hanging lamp in the middle of the saloon with his hands up.

"Todd, I know you won't shoot an unarmed man. So go on back to Dodge City until I can hire more and better help. I'll send for you again."

"No, Ezra, that's not going to happen. You're going to commit suicide like your cowardly brother."

Rex positioned himself so he could see Ezra in the mirror behind the bar as he turned his back on him to pull up a chair. As he expected, Ezra's hand darted into his inside pocket. The Henry blew him off his feet.

Ezra looked wide-eyed at Rex, "You … you …"

"I knew you'd commit suicide."

Rex walked out of the saloon and went in search of Sissy.

BOOMERANG

Matt Harding, along with three other passengers, boarded the stage in Helena bound for Deadwood several hours earlier. They would soon arrive at the stage waystation nearest Deadwood on the Helena trail but the normal half-hour stop for a change of horses and a hot meal would certainly be extended. The clouds rolling in from Canada and which they had been watching with some concern for the past hour had opened up and was releasing snow at an alarming rate. The horses, now nearly exhausted, had been pushed to the limit. When they pulled up in front of the waystation Matt noticed George, the station manager, carrying in firewood from a covered shelter near the station. He soon returned to assist the passengers inside and then rush the horses into the barn.

Upon entering the waystation the passengers saw a huge fireplace going at full blast trying to warm, as much as possible, the large entry room. There were several easy chairs spread around the room with a large, rectangular table in the middle now being set for eight passengers. A few feet on the other side of the table and across from the fireplace was a small bar. Beside the bar was a hall that ran to a door leading out of the station. About thirty feet behind that door was the barn which accommodated a sufficient number of horses to provide fresh teams to service two stages daily.

This had been the first time Mark had taken time from his job as deputy marshal of Deadwood. Mark, not a social animal, traveled to

Helena to serve as his cousin's best man and had attended all of the functions thereby required. He was happy for his cousin but somewhat sad that at the age of almost thirty he had not yet experienced a serious romantic relationship.

Further, he felt awkward without his sidearm and badge which he had left in Deadwood because he reasoned they would be out of place at a wedding.

Upon entering the station, Mark discovered that the passengers on the incoming stage from Deadwood had also taken refuge. The station manager informed everyone that while there was plenty of food for the emergency, since the station was not equipped for overnight lodging, sleeping arrangements would be decided later. He also announced that the bar would be open for those so inclined and that a meal would be served shortly.

The drivers and guards were served at a table in the kitchen while the eight passengers were seated at a large rectangular table in the great room. When the food was brought out it was apparent that George's wife was an excellent cook.

George, a big man in his fifties, approached Matt whom he had known for some time and handed him an envelope whispering, "Matt, this was sitting on the bar. I haven't opened it but since the outside says it must be read to the passengers immediately, I leave it up to you."

Matt opened the envelope and read the note inside. It was a prime example of good penmanship. It showed the writer took pride in the handwriting. But it also raised a question: did the writer have a sense of humor or did he bear a grudge? Was this a joke or was it a threat? Matt decided to let the passengers decide.

After everyone was seated at the table, Matt asked for their attention.

"I have somethin' to read to you. It was left at the bar without any indication of who prepared it. It may just be a joke to provide entertainment for our forced stay here or it may be an actual threat. Here's what the note says:

'Welcome. We are about to engage in a game, a game of life or death. You see, one of us is going to be murdered within the next hour and equally outrageous, one of us will be the murderer. Now what should we do? We can't each go to our room for none of us have rooms. Certainly we don't want to sit outside alone in a South Dakota winter. Since there would appear to be safety in numbers, perhaps we should just sit here and watch each other. How will the threat be carried out, shooting, poisoning, stabbing, a blunt instrument? The game is indeed getting' interesting. One of us must take the lead in determining who the proposed victim is and who the potential killer is. Perhaps determining one will determine the other, perhaps not. The hour is running."

"The writer is correct," said Matt.

"We must assume the note means what it says. So we need to determine which of us is at risk. Unless someone else wants to job, I'll take the lead."

A man sitting across the table spoke up." That seems fitting, Deputy Harding."

"Do you know me?"

"No but I know of you." The speaker was about Matt's height of six feet but slightly heavier. He was dressed in a suit and was well spoken. "I'm Bryan Griffin and I'm a salesman who frequently calls on Deadwood. Your newspaper loves to play up your exploits. They carried a picture of you not long ago. They compare you with some fictional detective from London called Sherlock who uses deductive reasoning instead of guns and bullets to solve crimes."

"Oh, I carry a firearm when I'm workin' and it's loaded. It's just that a gun doesn't help you to think or reason. Do you know anyone else in the group?"

"I don't really know them but I met them since we all came out on the Deadwood stage this morning. There's Abe Lawson sitting at the end of the table next to you. Then there's Miss Le Fay sitting on my right and Bill Ernest sitting on the other side of her."

"Miss Le Fay, what were you doin' in Deadwood?"

A beautiful woman in her late twenties, perhaps too flamboyantly dressed, responded, "If you were old enough to frequent the Miner's Saloon, Deputy, you'd know. I work there."

"And why are you on this stage?"

"I needed a change of scenery."

"And you, Sir, why were you in Deadwood?"

"Like Mr. Griffin, I'm a salesman just completing my route."

'And you, Mr. Lawson?"

"I live in Deadwood, actually on a ranch outside of town. Like Mr. Griffin, I've also read about you in the local newspaper."

"It's interestin' that all of you from the Deadwood stage are sittin' side by side. Of course, those of us from the Helena stage also are. Now for the Helena stage. As indicated, I'm Matt Hardin', deputy marshal of Deadwood. I've been to Helena attendin' a weddin'. Let me introduce the others to the Deadwood passengers. Dr. Ames is sittin' there at the end of the table opposite Mr. Lawson. Dr. Ames, what has put you on this stage?"

Ames, tall and very thin with a beard popularized by Abe Lincoln, responded, "Well, after practicing medicine for the last twenty years in Virginia City, most often the only medical care in town, I decided to retire when a new doctor moved in. I'm looking for a new place to settle. I checked out Helena for a while and now I'm going to look at Deadwood."

"And to Dr. Ames' left is Mrs. Sadie Horton." Mrs. Horton, dark haired and still attractive at forty although she was getting heavy and her hair showed signs of gray, answered Matt's question as to why she was on the stage.

"My husband recently died and I'm looking for a place to get away from depressing memories. I hope Deadwood will be such a place."

"Sitting to her left is Roy Arnold. Roy, why are you here?"

"It's no mystery. I work for the Abbot mining company in Deadwood and I've been to Helena on its business. I'm now going home."

Dr. Ames, with a curious smile on his face asked, "Deputy, is it significant that we have aligned ourselves according to the stage we were on?"

"It may be. Of course it is probable that one will sit next to someone he or she has known even for a day"

"What else have you concluded?"

"I have reached a tentative conclusion, perhaps not from deductive reasonin' as much as from observation and common sense, but then again perhaps that is deductive reasonin'. Anyway I suggest the prospective killer and the potential victim arrived on the same stage. That alone doesn't solve the puzzle or end the game, but it may assist. We can now examine carefully the passengers on one stage and see what unfolds."

Dr. Ames again, "What has led you to the conclusion that a single stage carried both the potential killer and the intended victim?"

"First, the game itself is too well conceived to have been devised on the spot after arrivin' here. Second, the note given me to read was clearly prepared before the stage ride. No one on our stage, and I reasonably assume on the other, could have written so legibly with the bumpy ride we encountered. Finally, in the note the writer referred to 'sitting outside in a South Dakota winter.' I see this as too general under the circumstances. The note would have said 'South Dakota blizzard' had the writer foreseen it. No, the game was planned and the note written after the writer knew a certain passenger, his or her prey, would be on board this stage. Therefore, who among us has provoked such outrage as to cause this reaction from an enemy?"

"It's probably me."

Everyone turned to look at the speaker, Miss LeFay.

Matt looked at her carefully, "And why would you say that?"

"It's embarrassing, Deputy."

"Ma'am, would you rather be embarrassed or dead? I will tell you now that whatever you or anyone answers to my questions will not be used against you."

"Well, my name is actually Wilma Brown, LeFay is my professional name. It appears that I became too close both physically and emotionally, to a . . . client. I fell in love with him and he returned my affection."

"And what's wrong with that?"

"He is married and his wife is the daughter of the richest and most influential miner in the area. She convinced her father that I should be run out of town. A ticket for this stage was delivered to me two days ago and the enclosed note informed me that if I didn't leave dire things would happen to me. I discussed it with Harold, the man involved, and he encouraged me to go. He planned to meet me in Helena in three days. He had some matters to finish up. I was informed just before the stage left that Harold was allegedly set upon by drunks and was beaten so badly he is expected to be in the hospital for days."

"Allegedly? You don't believe it?"

"Not for a minute."

"And the wife's father would be Randolph Wilkes?"

"He's the one."

"And you believe that runnin' you out of town may not satisfy his anger?

"They must have discovered that Harold intended to join me and they made that impossible, at least for a while. Now I fear they may want to make me unavailable for him to ever meet."

Matt looked at Mr. Griffen, "Who is your employer?"

"That won't be necessary, Deputy. My name isn't Griffin. It's Bert Wilkes. Because we run in different circles, I knew you wouldn't recognize me. I also know that if anything happens to Miss Brown you will investigate our family carefully and I would be discovered. I think it better to speak now. I was sent along to make sure Miss Brown goes to Helena and stays there."

"And that's all there is to it?"

"She might have run into someone who changed her appearance some. Not me, but someone. That is all"

"Can I assume that nothing will happen to her in Helena?"

"Deputy, I am ashamed that our family did not stand up to my sister. It will not happen again. Miss Brown will be safe in Helena or Deadwood if she chooses to return.

"Miss Brown, I am truly sorry."

"Mr. Wilkes, I accept your word that no harm will come to Miss Brown and I know you are not the potential killer we are looking for since I don't think you came up with this game."

"Its's a stupid game; If someone means to harm another, why warn him?

"Why, indeed?"

"Dr. Ames, I am so troubled by one of your previous statements that I doubt you are a doctor, that you have ever been in Virginia City, and that Ames is your name."

Now smiling broadly, the erstwhile Dr. Ames responded, "You're right on every point. My name isn't Ames, I'm not a doctor, and I've never been in Virginia City. It has reached that point in the game when my role needs be revealed. But what gave me away?"

"Nothing dramatic, it's just that I have been in Virginia City. My family lived there when I was younger. I do not recall ever hearing of a Dr. Ames and in a place as small as Virginia City that would be odd. And I know that for years Virginia City's medical needs were admirably met by a clinic operated by Catholic Sisters."

"I do have a reason for my deception which will become apparent. Mrs. Horton, however, was even more deceptive. While I was in Helena I read the newspapers. She was featured even more than you. Her husband did not merely die, he was murdered and she and her banker- boyfriend were charged with that murder."

"I was acquitted of that charge," Mrs. Horton quickly retorted.

"We'll get to that in a minute. Her first statement to the police was that she was out the evening that it happened and an intruder must have come in and shot her husband. He was, after all, a lawyer who had made many enemies. For a while it looked as though this story would work but then someone suggested to the police that Mrs. Horton was having an affair with a local banker, Jeff Bates. When the investigator approached Mrs. Horton about her obvious lie, she had another ready. It is true she was having an affair but when she told Mr. Bates that she was going back to her husband, Bates decided to kill him.

"When Mr. Bates learned of her statement blaming him he became highly agitated. The mere accusation cost him his job and his wife so he had no reason not to make a full confession. Bates stated that when her husband found out about their affair he was going to divorce her and because of her adultery she would receive nothing.

"She went to Bates and told him that his name would certainly be raised in the divorce case and his only chance to prevent his ruination was to kill her husband before he could file it.

She would be out of the house and he could be an intruder who broke in and killed her husband. No one knew about their affair so there was no risk. She said she had no idea how her husband found out or how the police learned about them."

Matt asked Mrs. Horton's accuser. "Do you know how the police found out?"

Sheepishly he responded, "As a matter of fact. I do. My name is Heath Horton and I am the husband's father. My son and I had a serious falling out many years ago when I divorced his mother and married a younger woman. We didn't speak for years but I was able through lawyer friends to stay aware of his location. And I knew that after his first wife died, he married a woman fifteen years younger than he. When my second wife died last year I decided to try to make amends with my son. So I went to Helena. The day before my son was murdered I went by his office hoping he would see me. He was receptive. After a clumsy beginning we had a good meeting and I thought reconciliation was possible. He couldn't invite me to his home, he said, because he had just discovered his wife was having an affair with a local banker and he told her he would divorce her and she would get nothing.. He was preparing the papers for the divorce which he hoped to file within a week. As I said, he was murdered that evening.

"When it appeared the police were unaware of this fact, I wrote an anonymous note so advising them."

Matt looked at Heath Horton. "Would I be wrong to suggest you are Judge Heath Horton who used to serve this area by riding the circuit? I believe you were called Harsh Horton because of your harsh sentences. I never saw you before but people say you demanded the most from the parties, the lawyers and yourself."

"Yes I was once a Judge."

With that Judge Horton reached into his suit pocket and pulled out a revolver which he laid on the table facing Mrs. Horton with his hand covering it and his finger near the trigger

"Judge, you don't intend to shoot Mrs. Horton, do you?"

"Patience, my friend, first I want to advise her that she will not receive a dime of the fortune my son and his first wife accumulated. Most states have now passed what is known as 'slayer statutes' which prevent one who is involved in the intentional killing of a person to inherit from that person."

Mrs. Horton again interposed, "But I was acquitted and my lawyer says I can't be tried again for his death."

"It's true that the criminal court is through with you. But inheritance is a civil matter based on different principles and a different standard of proof. Here, the judge and not a jury may still determine by a greater weight of the evidence that you were involved the killing which was unlawful and intentional and apply the slayer statute to you. Now I as his father and his only legal next of kin have had my lawyer petition the court for an order barring you from any access to my son's estate."

"And what would you have me do, become a saloon woman like Miss Brown there?"

"No, I want you living on the street penniless, helpless, hopeless, and alone."

The Judge looked distracted by someone behind him; he removed his hand from the revolver and looked away. In that instant, Mrs. Horton grabbed the gun and pointed it at the Judge.

"Don't believe I can't use this. You will not live to see me penniless and with you dead, no one can challenge me.

She fired and the bullet entered the Judge's chest. The Judge looked at Matt and held up one finger before he fell.

"Matt rose from the table and, after making sire the Judge was dead, approached Mrs. Horton. You're under arrest for the murder of Judge Horton."

"Don't come any nearer this gun has six bullets."

"I believe it's empty.

She fired the gun again. Click. Again, click.

"Matt took the gun from her. "Now we'll add a count of attempted murder to your charges."

Bert Wilkes asked, "How did you know there were no more bullets?"

"The Judge told me when he held up one finger. He only put one bullet in the gun so no one else would get harmed."

"Why the game?"

"The Judge thought of the game to put ultimate pressure on Mrs. Horton. He didn't want her to get away with murder again so if she murdered him the law might do better. He goaded her with the loss of her inheritance to push her over."

Miss. Brown continued, "It's a shame that the judge's plan to shoot Mrs. Horton boomeranged.

Matt responded, "There was no boomerang. The Judge never intended to shoot her. He was from the beginning the intended victim.

After getting statements from everyone in attendance and the weather cleared enough for the stage to depart for Deadwood Mrs. Horton sat beside the body of the Judge all the way to Deadwood.

COBRA

Ben Hatch had finished lunch and was walking out of the Virginia City Diner when he spotted the young man standing a few feet away apparently waiting for him. Ben had not seen the man before but he knew full well what he had in mind. This would be three times in three months he'd been confronted by an ambitious gunman and it was getting tiresome. The man, kid really, had the earmarks of one who wished to enhance his reputation as a gunman by outdrawing a legend. That's where Ben came in.

The kid followed Ben who was headed to his rooming house a short distance away. Finally, when there appeared enough people on the street to make a sizable audience, Ben heard what he expected, "That's far enough, Cobra. Let's see how good you are." Ben had a routine he had developed for these wannabe gunmen.

"Kid, you don't know me so it can't be anythin' personal?"

"That's right."

"And I've never seen you so I have no reason to kill you. It must be that you believe that if you're able to outshoot me, my reputation will automatically flow to you."

"Isn't that the way it works?"

"Only if you want a shortcut and that's a dangerous route. Why'd you choose me?

"There are four of us in Cheyenne who've practiced together for years. We practice drawin' and shootin' and we're almost equal. We all want to be the best around but we don't want to kill each other to prove it. Besides shootin someone about as good as you doesn't make a reputation but shootin someone with a good reputation does. We have a list of possible names and your name's on it. You became questionable because you're gettin' old and killin' someone past his prime has less reputation value. But then you killed a young gunman two weeks ago. My cousin who's a deputy here wrote that you looked like the old Cobra who's draw is as quick and deadly as it ever was. I didn't tell my friends 'cause I want you all to myself."

"I should tell you you're greatly outclassed. Go back to Cheyenne."

"I have two reasons to be confident I'll win. First, you're twenty years older than when you got your reputation. There's even gray in your hair. Second, you've tried so hard to talk me out of a gun fight proves you've lost your nerve."

The kid went for his gun. He was pretty good but still his revolver hadn't cleared his holster when the Cobra struck.

Ben looked around to see who had witnessed the shootout.

"Sam. You heard and saw everythin'. Tell the marshal since he'll need a statement for the record."

Ben continued on to his rooming house. When he was in his room, he took a valise from his closet and packed his few belongings. He left his revolver and his gun belt in his room.. To kill kids barely out of their teens was more than even a hardened gunman could accept. There must be a better way.

Bill Hickok's solution to kids who wanted to kill him because of his reputation was to live out loud in Deadwood. He figured most of the ambitious ones would want to live and would weigh their chances carefully. But a gunman's danger is not always from a shootout.

Hickok was shot in the back of the head while he was engaged in a friendly poker game.

Ben decided on a different plan. He would simply disappear for a while. He would change his location, his name and his habits. When he was working for some cattlemen over near the South Dakota border to ward off rustlers he became aware of a small town that he believes will meet his needs to hide away.

The next morning he boarded a stagecoach for Badger Crossing.

***

Ben walked up to the reception desk of the Badger Hotel and faced a short, rotund and very friendly clerk.

"I'm Will Holt and you're . . .?"

Ben had decided on a new name.

"I'm Harry Pillow."

"You be here a while?"

"It depends. I'm lookin' for work."

"Well I think some of the ranches around her are hirin'. I know Mrs. Watson who owns the hardware store says she needs help. But I have to warn you. her husband was killed a few months ago when their store was robbed.. The robber came in just after openin'. No one can figure why he was shot since Al didn't wear a gun and would not have resisted. He must have known the robber."

"An even bigger question might be the timing of the robbery. My father owned a hardware store in a small town near Bannack and I worked for him until I moved on. There'd be very little money in the register until later in the day, just the money put in by the owner to start business. I suppose it could be that the robber was so unhappy to find no money that he shot the owner. But I doubt it."

"Go ahead and register, Mr. Pillow, and I'll take you luggage to your room if you'd like to call on Mrs. Watson before she closes for the day."

Ben accepted the clerk's offer and found the hardware store only a few doors down and across the street.

Ben entered the store and saw a handsome woman near his age, about forty, behind the counter. Because it was near closing time, no one else was present.

"Mrs. Watson, I'm Harry Pillow and I am advised you may be looking for help. If so, I'd like to apply."

"Well you seem large enough, about the size of my late husband, I'd say about six feet and a hundred eighty. You need to be pretty strong to move much of our merchandise around. Are you familiar with the hardware business?"

"When I was a kid I worked in my father's store."

"I see you don't carry a gun. Is there a reason?"

"I've decided carrying a gun makes no sense. If you're not the best gunman alive, in any given gunfight you may be the worst. Since you can't always choose your opponent, I've decided to avoid them all."

"I wish you'd explain that to my seventeen-year-old son, Billy. Since my husband was killed in the robbery, Billy and his best friend have started to carry guns. Under the circumstances, I find it difficult to refuse him the opportunity to defend himself."

"I hope he gets very good or remains lucky."

"Concerning the job, it's your if you want it. It's part time, you'll start at 8:00 opening time and work until noon. After I clean the family quarters upstairs, I'll help downstairs. I pay one half a cowboy's wages and provide room and board. My husband built a bedroom in the back of the storage section for his father which has an outside entrance. Breakfast is a 7:30 in my kitchen upstairs with lunch served at noon after I've relieved you. Dinner will be at 6:30. You start in the morning."

***

Ben was surprised to find he enjoyed his new job. The people in the community were friendly and inclusive. They asked him to join them for a friendly poker game in the evenings at seven o'clock in the "Feel Good" Saloon. No one drank much no one won or lost much. The game would last for one hour, it was low stakes and no professional gamblers were invited. It was a chance for the businessmen of the community to socialize with other businessmen after a day's work. Ben was curious about who killed Mr. Watson and he knew the best place to learn about the town and its people would be in a local card game. He accepted.

***

Some weeks after he came to Badger Junction, Ben, Billy and Mrs. Watson were having dinner upstairs. Billy's mind seemed somewhat occupied and he did not participate in the conversation. Mrs. Watson turned to Ben and asked, "Will you tell Billy what you told me about the wisdom of wearing a gun?"

"Mrs. Watson, I'd rather not interfere with your relationship with Billy. He'll have to decide for himself."

"Please. He should at least consider it."

"Well, Billy, what I told your mother is that if you wear a gun you're advertising that you are willing to use it and you're implying that you can use it well. If you are out one night and inadvertently offend someone, he may call you out. Your honor is now at stake and most people would be forced to accept the challenge. Or suppose someone deliberately offends you. He will expect you to call him out. Again, it becomes a matter of honor. In either event, one of you may die over the most insignificant matter."

Billy looked hard at Ben, "Mr. Pillow, that sounds like a coward's response. Mother, I have a question. I know Mr. Pillow's board is part of his salary but must we eat with the hired help?"

"Billy!"

"He's right, Mrs. Watson. Meals should be with family. I have no objection to eating in my room."

"Well, I object. If Billy doesn't want to eat with adults, he can take his dinner to his room. Besides, I like talking to you."

Billy glared at Ben, picked up his plate and left the room. A few minutes, later they heard him leave.

Mrs. Watson looked sadly at Ben, "Since his father's death, Billy has become impossible. I can't understand it."

"Perhaps he feels I'm competin' with him for your affection."

"Perhaps, I guess. Are you?"

"Perhaps."

"I was talking to some of the wives of men you play poker with. They think a lot of you. They are considering running you for president of the business owner's group."

"I don't own a business."

"They're willing to change the rules."

"I'd better get to the poker game now," he said walking toward the door.

***

Ben was sitting in the poker game beside Foster Blake. He had just drawn three aces when he heard Foster whisper, "Harry, you boss's son and his friend just came in. I'll bet Helen doesn't approve of him being here."

As Ben watched, Billy turned to his friend and ran headlong into Preston Longacre. Half of Longacre's beer spilled to the floor and Longacre gave Billy a responding shove almost sending him down. In a reflex action, Billy pushed back.

"How about that. The hardware kid has challenged me, and he's wearin' a gun.

"Timmy," Longacre said to his friend beside him, "another hardware man is about to make the news."

Longacre let his hand linger above his gun as he said to Billy, "When you're ready, Kid."

Ben could see Billy was torn between walking out of the saloon to be forever branded a coward and going for his gun. Ben was afraid of the choice Billy might make.

From the poker table a voice sounded. It was so quiet it could hardly be heard but it was heard and it had the impact of a shout.

"Leave the kid alone."

"Who said that? Who has the nerve to interfere in my business? Stand if you have the courage."

Ben stood facing Longacre. To deflect attention from Billy, Ben responded, "You want me to repeat it, halfwit? You can go home now and live."

"And insulting also. Why do I get a green kid who's about to throw up with fright and an insulting old cowboy who hasn't the nerve to wear a gun belt? You'll have to wait, Cowboy, your lack of a gun saved you this time. Now I need to get back to the boy."

Ben turned to Foster, "Loan me your gun belt, please."

As Foster unbuckled his gun belt, he whispered to Ben, "Longacre is rumored to be very good with a gun. Do you know anything about guns?"

"Enough."

Longacre watched Ben strap on the gun belt, remove the revolver, spin the cylinder to assure the gun was fully loaded, and then firmly and quickly return the gun to the holster.

"When you're ready, halfwit."

"Timmy, the cowboy pretends he's used a gun before. Should I be scared? Cowboy, tell the folks in here who you were before I killed you."

The men at the poker table were surprised when their friend said softly, "My name is Ben Hatch."

"Well, Mr. Hatch, I've never heard of you."

A voice from the end of the bar spoke up. "I now remember where I know him from. Longacre, if he gives you another chance to leave and save your life, take it. He's as much better than you than you are the kid."

"How do you know the Old Man?"

'I lived in Bullock twenty or so years ago. The town had just hired a young and cocky deputy named Hatch. He immediately gained the reputation as being the fastest deputy we ever had. He was said to be even faster than our outlaw lawman, Sheriff Plummer, who was said to be able to draw and fire three shots within three seconds.

"One day Hatch was on his way to the bank to deposit his first deputy pay check. when he encountered three men. The men had just robbed the bank, made the employees and customers lay on the floor and told them if they made a sound for two minutes they'd come back and kill them. The men then holstered their weapons and casually walked out of the bank headed for their horses.

"There they were, three robbers on the boardwalk just outside the bank and the deputy in the street about to climb the stairs up to the boardwalk when an employee sounded the alarm. Awareness came to all at the same time and each man went for his gun. Two robbers died before they could get off a shot. The third fired a shot but it was so rushed it missed everything. There was no second chance.

"Hatch glanced at the bodies and went into the bank, made sure the people inside were all right, and made his deposit.

"A reporter was at the scene immediately and questioned the bystanders. The next day, an article appeared in our paper that said the robbers had no chance against our deputy who's draw is as quick and deadly as a cobra strike. He was referred to as Cobra after that."

"That may be but as you said that was twenty years ago. I was four years old at the time. I've grown up and he's grown old. Look at his gray hair." With that, Longacre went for his gun.

Longacre came in second as two bullets plowed into his chest.

Ben walked up to Timmy, "Sit at that table over there, I want to talk to you." Ben followed Timmy to the table and they talked quietly.

"Tim, I saw the look that went between you and Longacre when he mentioned that a second hardware man was about to make the news. It appeared to be a private joke between you. I think Longacre killed Watson. I want to know why."

Timmy thought a minute. "I don't know why I shouldn't tell you now. Mr. Watson was seein' another man's wife. The husband found out and paid Preston to end the romance."

"How do you know?"

"Preston was paid a sum up front with a balance due when the job was done. He asked me to go with him to collect the final payment. He wanted a witness in case he decided later to seek more money from the husband."

"And who was that husband?"

"Doctor Ames. He's old, fat, and rich but his wife is young, beautiful and bored."

Ben stood to leave, "Timmy, stay away from Billy and I won't kill you."

Ben returned to his poker group and returned the gun belt to its owner. He then looked in turn at each of them. "The only lie I told you was my name. I'm sorry I lied to you. I've just killed a man barely out of his teens. Now I need to be alone for a while."

***

Helen Watson was disturbed about Billy's behavior at the dinner table. Earlier she had intended to talk to him but he was not in his room. Now she heard sounds reflecting he had returned home. This was as good a time as any.

She knocked on his door and it was immediately opened. His eyes were red as though he had been crying.

"Billy, what's wrong?"

"I called him a coward."

"Who?"

"Mr. Pillow. Momma, he's the bravest man who ever lived. He killed a man tonight to save my life."

To keep from falling, she sat on the bed.

"Billy, tell me about it."

"Momma, I knew you wouldn't like it so I picked up Winston and we went to the saloon to see what goes on there. When we entered the saloon, I accidently bumped this fellow and he spilled his beer. He became very upset with me and pushed me. He pushed me in front of

Winston. I had to push him back. This really made him mad and he said I had challenged him and he accepted. He squared up to draw. Momma, I didn't know what to do except I knew I couldn't back down even though I knew I'd lose.

"We were about to draw when Mr. Pillow told him to leave me alone."

"This made Longacre madder at Pillow than at me. They had a few words and Mr. Pillow borrowed a gun belt and faced Longacre. It turns out that Mr. Pillow's name isn't Pillow, it's Ben Hatch. And he's probably the fastest gun in Montana.

"I heard him come in just a few minutes ago."

"You did, did you? He lied to me about his name and about his experience with a gun and Lord only knows what else. Let's go to his room and find out."

Ben answered the door knock and saw Mrs. Watson and Billy standing there.

"Mrs. Watson?"

"Dammit, call me Helen." She put her arms around his neck, pulled him forward and kissed him hard on the lips.

"That's for saving Billy's life."

Helen stepped back a pace and swung her open hand as hard as she could slapping Ben across the face.

"On the other hand, that's for telling me so many lies."

Ben rubbed his face and grinned, "To tell you the truth. I prefer your thanks to your 'on the other hands'."

Helen also smiled.

"Actually, the only lie I told you was my name and I had a reason for that."

"How about the fact that you weren't good with a gun?"

"All I said was that I found it made no sense to carry a gun because it would only get you in trouble. Okay, I only quit carrying a gun shortly before I met you. But I didn't say when I gave it up.

"Billy probably told you I have a reputation as a fast gun. It has its downside. Young men wantin' an instant reputation as a gunman will flock to have a go with a recognized gunman. Countin' the young man tonight, I've killed several this year. I'm fed up with it. I decided to come here, change my name, get a job, and try to fit in. Perhaps they wouldn't find me."

"Why here?"

"I worked for a cattlemen's group protectin' their herds against rustlers not far from here. I came here a few times. Anyway, after tonight they'll know where I am and start comin' again. I'll have to move on."

Helen looked at him, "I don't want you to go."

Billy added, "I don't want you to go either. Especially when I'm moving to Deadwood. I sorta hoped you'd look after Momma."

"Billy!"

"Mom, everyone knows how he looks at you. He might as well look after you too."

"Why ae you going to Deadwood, Billy? I see you're not wearing your gun belt."

"I put it back in inventory. My uncle manages a gold operation there and has offered to teach me the mining business. It's a great opportunity."

"Yeah, it certainly is. Let's talk about the other thing tomorrow."

***

It was two weeks after the shootout with young Longacre. Foster Blake and his wife were hosting Ben and Helen for a Saturday afternoon lunch. Billy had moved to Deadwood to start his training under his uncle's supervision and Ben had delayed making a decision on relocating, hoping the problem would just go away. It did not.

There was a knock on the door and the marshal was invited in.

"Ben, a young gunman anxious to take on the Cobra came to town this morning. He came by the jail asking where the Cobra lived. I told him you didn't live here anymore. He grumbled some and rode off. But not very far. I decided you should know and since I knew you and Helen were having lunch with Foster I came here. The gunman followed me and is outside now. He says he just wants to talk to you and I can't think of a reason to arrest him. I'm sorry."

"Marshal, it had to happen. I've decided on a new tactic so keep a close watch on the young gunman. Foster, I want to purchase your gun belt and revolver. How much?"

"I'll just loan it to you again."

"This time I won't be returning it."

Foster handed him the gun belt. "We'll talk price later."

The marshal and Ben walked out of the house and over to where the gunman waited. Helen and the Blakes followed them out.

The gunman looked at Ben appraisingly. "So you're the Cobra."

"No, I used to be but I quit."

"You can't quit."

"Sure I can. I'm not gun fightin' anymore. Unless you want to be the Cobra, he's dead."

Ben unbuckled the gun belt and folded it with the revolver inside. He then tossed it at the gunman's feet. "That's the body of the Cobra for you to do with as you please." Ben turned to walk away.

"Not so fast," said the gunman. "Take another step and it'll be your last one."

The marshal drew his revolver and faced the gunman, "Young man, if I even think you're going for your gun, I'll drop you where you are."

The gunman looked at Ben and appeared helpless and confused, "You don't mind being called a coward?"

"Not at all. Ben went inside.

The gunman bent over and picked up the discarded gun belt.

"Well, I suppose the Cobra's revolver might make a good trophy." He got on his horse and rode away.

A REUNION OF FRIENDS

"Wally" Wallace sat alone near the swinging entry doors of the Royal Flush Saloon. He'd spent most of the day riding over from Longview and, he admits to himself, is somewhat apprehensive. But he can handle himself in a saloon brawl and better than good with his revolver should shooting break out. Further, his experience in law enforcement for the past ten years has given him the maturity most thirty-year-olds lack.

Across the room from him is the bar occupied by only two men. Wally's interest in them became aroused because they had been there for as long as he, which was about thirty minutes, and have been nursing their drinks the whole time. Not just nursing, they hadn't touched them.

This, he thought, is unusual behavior for cowboys.

It was still early for the night's crowd, only two saloon girls working and no card games in progress. He is here to meet a friend and to help with such troubles his friend may be encountering. His friend, Adam Clay, saved his life five years ago when they were both deputies in Cheyenne, Wyoming. It was in a saloon such as this. When Wally was arresting a drunken patron who started a brawl, the patron's companion decided to take Wally out. Adam, new at the job and totally inadequate with a gun, intervened. He prevented Wally from being shot from behind but in the process was himself shot in the leg. Adam realized law enforcement was not for him. He decided ranching was safer.

Wally eventually went on to marshal a small mining town, Longview, just north of the Wyoming border. When he was hired he was told to clean up the town so decent people would be safe. He did so only to find that a safe town would not attract the miners and trail hands who could choose among other small towns to spend their money. Safety, he was told, had to accommodate business. He was terminated with the appreciation of the mayor for a job well done. It was at this time that he received Adam's letter.

Adam and his sister had grown up with Wally in Cheyenne on a nearby ranches. Adam and his sister, now a widow, purchased a ranch up in the Big Horn Valley after the government, following Custer's inglorious defeat, moved the Indians back to their reservations. Adam informed him that he was facing serious trouble and needed Wally's help.

Wally was available so he immediately responded.

On the way to the Royal Flush, he stopped at Adam's ranch only to find Adam had gone to meet with the source of his trouble and would meet Wally at the saloon afterwards. Adam's sister, Helen, was concerned about the safety of her brother. He had this on-going problem with Henry Dooley, their up-stream neighbor. Dooley, who first tried unsuccessfully to buy their property, dammed the stream cutting off their access to water for their cattle. Because the law was clear that an up-stream owner can't deprive those down-stream from access to water, Adam sued in the federal court in Helena and felt confident he would prevail.

There had recently been a hearing in the case and they were awaiting the judge's decision. Dooley must have doubts about his position because he requested this meeting. The problem Adam faced was that court proceedings sometimes take a long time and cattle can't go on forever without water. Ponds on his property had

118

provided temporary relief but they wouldn't last during the summer season.

After the meeting, regardless of whether a settlement was reached, Adam and Dooley agreed to go by the Royal Flush and have a drink to the health of the other to show no hard feelings. It was the civilized thing to do.

Adam's sister, two years younger than Adam, did not trust Dooley and wanted Adam to wait until Wally arrived. He refused. Adam and Dooley entered the saloon without noticing Wally who decided to remain in the back and quietly watch. He saw Dooley position himself at the bar so that Adam was standing next to the two men waiting there. He also noticed Dooley make eye contact with one of the men. The two men, Wally noticed, suddenly appeared intoxicated.

After Adam and Dooley were served their drinks, the redheaded "drunk" approached Adam and asked to buy him a whiskey. Adam refused looking down at the drink before him, "I have one."

The redhead picked up Adam's drink and poured it on the floor. "Now you don't."

"The answer if still no. Now, I simply don't want to drink with you."

In as slurred a voice as he could manage, the redhead proclaimed, "Now you're really insultin.' We'll see if you're fast enough to go around insultin' people.

The barman spoke up, "If you haven't noticed, he's not wearin' a gun. You shoot him, it's murder and around here we hang murderers."

The redhead turned to his comrade, "Joe, give him your gun."

By this time, Wally had approached the bar and pushed in between the redhead and Adam. "He won't need a gun. I have one."

"And who are you?"

"It's not important who I am. What you need to know is that I'm faster than you."

"There's two of us."

"I've taken that into account."

The redhead asked, "Do you know who I am?"

"It simply doesn't matter who you *are*. Very shortly you'll be dead and no one will care who you *were*."

Adam couldn't keep from laughing.

Joe spoke up, "What strikes you as funny?"

"You do, both of you, drunks who can't remember they're drunk. But if you draw against Wally Wallace, you'll be dead. That will be very funny."

The redhead looked at Wally. "You the former deputy of Cheyenne?"

"I've been a deputy and a marshal. Right now I'm just a man waitin' for you to draw so I can end this unpleasant matter and quietly have a drink with my friend."

"I have no argument with you. You didn't insult me like your friend did."

"I say you're a low-down, lyin' coward. Somewhere in that must be an insult as great as not havin' a drink with you."

"Joe, let's walk. We'll get 'im later."

As they walked away, Wally pushed Adam to the side, pulled his revolver and held it facing the departing "drunks." He waited. As he expected, Joe and the redhead spun around in unison with their guns in hand. He shot them before they could get off a shot.

Adam inquired, "How'd you know they'd do that?"

"It's an old trick that occasionally works. I thought they might try it. You walk away makin' your adversary think it's all over so he relaxes and lets down his guard. You turn and fire before he can react.

It's a trick mostly played on amateurs. I'm insulted. The response is to have your revolver ready when they start their turn. Mr. Dooley, you should really hire better help."

Dooley, a short, heavy man with a receding hair line responded, "You're not suggesting I had something to do with this?"

"More than suggestin,' Mr. Dooley, I'm accusin.' I saw you nod to the redhead just before the action started."

"I'm a friendly man, Mr. Wallace. I saw a stranger and nodded. He certainly doesn't work for me."

"I wouldn't expect him to be on your monthly payroll. It's more than likely a contract arrangement. From my experience in law enforcement, I'd expect a fair down payment was made with the balance being due tonight after the kill. Are you carryin' a lot of money tonight, Mr. Dooley?"

"You're crazy. Clay, I won't do business with anyone who has friends like this. My offer is withdrawn."

***

As they entered the ranch house they discovered Helen had prepared a late dinner.

"Since Wally is here, I knew things would go well and you'd want a big dinner."

"All did go well and I think our problem may be over," replied Adam, "and we appreciate the dinner."

"When I came by earlier, Helen, you were so upset about Adam, I didn't want to stay long enough to talk to you. Adam wrote me that Jesse had died. I'm sorry."

"Wally, that was well over two years ago. It's taken you a long time to express your condolence."

"I know and I'm sorry about that too. I'm not very experienced in this regard. I thought I'd see you and just express my regrets and you'd acknowledge it and it would be done. I didn't expect it to be this long before I saw you. I thought about writin' but if I wrioe you I'd be expected to say somethin' good about the deceased. I know there was a lot good about your husband. But since I made my play for you back in Cheyenne and came in second to Jesse, I couldn't think of what to say that didn't make me look like a sore loser, which I was. I figured you didn't want to marry a law officer because so many of us were being killed at the time and I thought that for me to express my sympathy might appear to be sayin 'see, ranchin' can be as dangerous as bein' a deputy.' Or worse, it could be seen as, 'look, now I have another chance.'"

"I'll accept your expressed regret as I'm sure it was intended. Thank you, Wally."

Over dinner, Adam explained his problem. "I think Helen told you the crux of it. Dooley offered to buy my ranch. I told him it was not for sale. He didn't like that answer so he's decided to cut off our water. When we couldn't resolve the matter, I sued and that made him even less happy. There was a summary hearin' on our complaint two weeks ago and we're waitin' for the judge to rule. At our meetin' tonight, he increased his offer dramatically. So much, in fact, that I might suggest to Helen that we consider it. Had those cowboys been successful tonight, his offer would be moot. You saved my life tonight so I guess that makes us even."

"No. Every day I live I owe to you. There's no getting' even when one saves your life.

"But I'm afraid you don't understand the danger. Those cowboys weren't tryin' to get even for your insult. They were paid to kill you and you're not out of danger yet."

"You really think Dooley paid them to kill me?"

"I do. I think Dooley's offer to you wasn't serious. He wanted you to feel good when you entered the saloon for what he intended to be your final drink. You notice he withdrew his offer in front of witnesses. What happens if the court doesn't rule fast enough?"

Helen spoke up, "If Dooley is intent on killing Adam, the court ruling may be worthless. What Adam needs is for you to stay."

Adam responded. "That would be the better answer but I have an alternative plan. John Blackwell owned the ranch just upstream from Dooley. He homesteaded it some time ago. He built a cabin and made the minimal required improvements sufficient to get the deed. He only cleared about thirty acres so it wouldn't be feasible to run cattle without doing much more clearing. What he did clear made good pasture and he has plenty of water."

"Where are you going with this?"

"Blackwell died and his daughter who lives in Denver inherited his ranch. I got her address from the lawyer who handled the estate and wrote her inquirin' whether she'd sell the property."

"Well, are you goin' to buy it or not?"

"Patience. I received a response saying she'll certainly consider it but since she's never seen her father's ranch, she wants to see it before she sells it. She'll be here on Friday's afternoon train. Since you're no longer a marshal, what do you intend to do?"

"I left ranchin' with my father when I was twenty because I wanted more excitement. Since I was good with a sidearm, the marshal offered me a job as deputy. I think I've had enough excitement now so I'll probably go back to ranchin'. My father says there's a ranch for sale next to his which I should consider."

Helen looked at him, "Why don't you consider the Blackwell property?"

"Because your brother wants to buy it. Besides, there appears to be a lot of work required to create a ranch out of the Blackwell property."

"Actually it might be a good idea for you to consider," said Adam. The price I'm sure will be most reasonable because the property has not been cleared and you're young enough that with a few helpers you can clear it in no time. Go with me when I meet the train."

***

Wally saw her step from the train. Because of her father's age when he died, Wally expected to see a woman in her forties. But this had to be the new owner because she was the only woman to get off the train. At most, she was in her early thirties. She had long brown hair and brown eyes, was stylishly slender and had a contagious smile. Wally felt mesmerized.

She was smiling at him. "Young man, you're staring at me and that's rude."

"I . . . yes, I was and I apologize. Since I don't know you, it's probably also rude to say you are the most beautiful women I've ever seen."

"Well even if it's rude, you need not apologize. Thank you. I am Sarah Westwood. Are you Adam?"

"No, I'm his friend, Wally. That's Adam approachin' now with the surrey. He just rented it to handle your luggage."

Adam brought the surrey as close as he could and he and Wally proceeded to load Sarah's luggage.

"Miss Westwood," said Adam seemingly unmoved by the woman's beauty, "my sister and I would like you to be our guest during your stay but if you would feel more comfortable in town, Wally and I will take you to the hotel."

"I accept your offer but, if possible, I'd like first to go by to see my probate lawyer, Arnold Sinclair. I have a loose appointment with him. I would like to learn the history of the property and, since I haven't seen my father for many years, learn something about him."

"Certainly, hop aboard and I'll take you there now."

"Adam," said Wally, "I'll go on back to the ranch and take your horse. Then I'll help Helen prepare for Miss Sarah."

Wally watched with some envy as Adam departed with Sarah.

Back at the ranch, Helen was full of questions.

"What does she look like? How did she react with you and Adam? Do you think she'll sell?"

"Wait a minute. Looks, she's about your height. Kind of skinny though. She was very friendly to both of us and she wanted to talk to the lawyer who handled the probate before discussin' a sale. She's goin' to be your guest so you'd better plan dinner."

To prepare for dinner, Helen chose four steaks and put four potatoes in the oven. While she was looking for something to make a salad, Wally moved his things out of the guest room.

Adam had only two full time ranch hands, hiring additional ones only when he needs more help such as roundups, herding to market and branding. His bunkhouse is large enough for another so Wally moved in there during Sarah's visit.

When Adam and Sarah came in, it was evident they had hit it off well.

"Sarah says she might just move out here. Wouldn't that be great?"

"Adam, you were going to try to buy her ranch, not encourage her to move onto it."

"If we buy her ranch, she'll move into town. She doesn't know anythin' about ranchin'."

Helen and Adam carried Sarah's bags into the guest room.

When they returned, Helen looked sternly at Wally, "You used to tell me I was the prettiest girl in the world. Now Adam tells me he overheard you say that to Sarah."

"I did not." When Wally saw Sarah looking at him, he added, "What I told Sarah is she's the most beautiful woman I've ever seen. When I spoke of your beauty, you were a girl. Sarah is a woman. Anyway, why does it matter now?"

"Because it shows how fickle you were."

"Me, fickle? You're the one who married someone else."

After dinner, Sarah discussed her life in Denver. "I've taught school in Denver for several years. My father and mother could not get along so he decided to homestead out here. That's when I was a young girl. He never came home so I never got to know him. I wish I had. I'm not happy with my job or my life in Denver so I was ready for a change when I heard from Adam about possibly buying the ranch. I decided to come out and see what a change of scenery might do. The probate lawyer was a friend of my father's and he gave me some insights as to what father was like. This trip has been a great experience so far."

They agreed to go see her ranch the following morning.

***

On the way to Sarah's ranch, Wally thought they were being followed. When they turned onto Sarah's ranch, the rider turned around. Wally decided to say nothing.

The part of the ranch Sarah's father had cleared gave great promise, but there was so little of it. The ranch house, unoccupied since her father's death, was reasonably clean and habitable. Sarah was delighted to see a picture of her as a very young girl on the mantle. Sarah's visit with the lawyer resulted in a recommended asking price for the ranch and Adam immediately accepted provided Sarah accompany him to the monthly Cattlemen's dance that evening. She accepted and the contract was agreed to.

Helen decided to go to the dance also and insisted Wally go should Adam encounter trouble from Dooley's people.

***

On the way to the dance, Adam announced he had received a wire that the judge had issued an injunction requiring the dam be removed within five days. Dooley will not be happy with that, he informed the group.

When they arrived at the dance, Wally excused himself from the others saying he wished to see if he recognized anyone there. The one he was looking for was Dooley and he was not yet there. It was still early.

Wally circulated through the crowd listening to the music and watching the dancers but always with Adam and Sarah in sight. The rider who had followed them this morning had put him on edge. It was easy to keep watch over Adam and Sarah because they were never apart. Until, that is, Adam left her alone to get her a punch.

Out on nowhere, Dooley and a young man approached Sarah. The young man was clearly a gunfighter, perhaps brought in by Dooley after the miserable showing of his previous gunmen. Wally worked his way through the crowd until he stood almost next to Dooley. He heard Dooley whisper to Sarah. "The lawyer says you may sell your ranch to Clay. I'll pay you more. You should keep that in mind because you'll not sell it to anyone but me. Accidents happen."

Wally interrupted Dooley in a loud voice intending to attract a crowd, "You seem to hire men to take care of people you don't like and yet you have no hesitation to threaten a young lady all by yourself. That takes courage."

Dooley appeared unfazed, "Mr. Wallace, I want you to meet my new foreman, Seth McCabe. He's better in many ways than the men you argued with in the saloon, men I never saw before."

McCabe spoke up, "Is this the man who spooked the strangers in the saloon? Wallace, if you've heard of me, you know I don't spook and I'm ready to take you on anytime."

"Probably anyone in law enforcement has heard of you, McCabe. What I heard is that as a gunman you rate in the second tier. When your master approves it, we'll compete. But Dooley needs to know this. If you draw on me, I'll kill you. If I believe that Dooley paid you to draw on me, I'll kill him too. Before you send Junior to fight for you, Dooley, know that your life depends on his ability."

McCabe squared up to draw; the crowd moved out of the line of fire.

"McCabe," said Dooley, "this is not the time or place. Too many people could get hurt."

"Yeah, including old man Wallace who's beyond his prime."

"That's one way to look at it. Another way is that even though at thirty I'm ten years older than you, I've had an additional ten years of practice. Junior, your hands are shakin'. Does that mean you're about to draw or that you're afraid to draw?"

Dooley grabbed McCabe's arm. "Can't you see he's baiting you? We're going now." Dooley almost had to pull McCabe out of the hall.

When Wally and the other three were together enjoying punch sitting on a bench outside the hall, Adam asked, "Wally, why'd you goad McCabe so much?"

"More than one reason. An experienced gunfighter once told me if you have an opportunity before an unavoidable gunfight, aggravate your opponent. Since he wants to kill you anyway, you have nothin' to lose. Show him he looks small in your eyes. He may rush his draw instead of his smooth, practiced draw. He'll have a tendency to jerk his gun out of his holster which may cause friction in the holster and slow down his draw. Even a fraction of a second can be the difference between life and death.

"Also why would I brag on my ability if I'm not really that good? Am I really faster than he is? This thought might also cause him to rush his draw. Finally, I wanted to cause some doubt in Dooley's mind as to how fast I am. That might come in handy."

On their way home from the dance, Wally pulled up beside the surrey to talk to Adam.

"I believe we have been followed from the hall. My guess it was McCabe and Dooley. One rider turned in at Dooley's ranch but one, almost certainly McCabe, is still following us. When we reach your entry, I'll jump from my horse and tie him to the surrey along with yours. Ride on up to the house and leave the surrey and our horses in plain view. Take the women inside and light a lamp only in the kitchen and all of you go into the parlor and keep quiet and low. Get your rifle and stay with the women until I come in. I'll let you know it's me.

From the front of the house, you can only see into the kitchen if you position yourself near the water trough. That's where I'll be lookin' for our guest. If I'm wrong about someone followin', I'll take care of the horses before I come in."

Because the one following stayed well back, Wally was confident he was trailing them more by sound and less by sight and would not notice Wally leave his horse. He found a place out of sight of one riding up to the ranch house and waited.

***

He heard the intruder before he saw him. But that was not unexpected. Even an Indian could not silently walk across the leaves and twigs which were deposited daily by the afternoon winds. The one approaching knew he was making noise but was confident he could not be heard from inside the ranch house.

The intruder approached the front of the house and, looking in, saw a lighted room revealing a portion of a table and a chair. The kitchen, he assumed. They're probably having a late snack or perhaps a nightcap. When they finish, one of the men, or perhaps both, will tend to the horses.

He saw the water trough in line with the window and the lamp and moved there to set up his vigil. He knelt behind the trough away from the house and rested his rifle on its top aimed at the front door.

Wally slipped up behind him. "Turn around and your dead."

The rifleman considered his options. Take a chance or spend a very long time in prison.

He opted for a trick he'd used before. Instead of turning, he simply fell over. This would normally delay a reaction from someone behind him. As he fell, he pointed the rifle in the direction of the voice and fired. He knew he'd missed when he felt a bullet enter his chest.

"McCabe, that trick works better if you start it from a standing position."

"I know," McCabe gasped, "but you caught me kneeling. I still got a shot off."

"I lied to you earlier. What I heard about you was that you were indeed an outstandin' gunman who always faced your opponent. I'm disappointed to find you're really a bushwhacker."

"I'm sorry too. And ashamed. And it's your fault. You seemed so sure of yourself that Dooley was afraid you'd beat me in a fair gunfight and then come for him. After Dooley threatened that woman tonight I just wanted to get away from him. He hadn't paid me yet to kill you and Clay and I needed the money to leave. He promised to pay for both of you if I killed either of you tonight.

"Dooley figured if I stayed close followin' you home I could get both of you when you came back from the barn after puttin' the horses away. When I saw you had gone inside to the kitchen leavin' the horses unattended, I figured all I had to do was wait. I picked a good place to get you both when you came out to move the horses."

"McCabe, if I let you lay here, you'll die. I can put you in that surrey and take you into town to a doctor but you'll probably die on the way. I'll do it if you want."

"That's considerate of you, but no, prison would be worse. What are you goin' to do about Dooley?"

"I don't know. If he carried a gun, I'd force him to draw against me. I suppose I'll have to be content with chargin' him with hirin' you to kill me."

"Without my testimony, I don't think you'll be able to convict him. I will share somethin' with you. He does carry a gun, a two shot Derringer. He keeps it under his coat. I saw him practice yesterday and within twenty feet he's deadly.I wish I could see you confront . . . " McCabe never said anything else.

***

Wally rode his horse to the front of Dooley's house figuring Dooley would think it was McCabe returning. A lamp was shining in the study off the entry way and Wally entered without knocking. He was glad for the poor lighting. He took about three paces when he heard Dooley behind him.

"I have a Derringer pointed at your back. Carefully turn around. I suppose since you're here, you killed McCabe."

Wally kept his hands raised as he turned around.

"Yeah, he was very upset when you wouldn't let him kill me at the dance. He was even more upset when you threatened the woman."

"I know; he complained about both. Can ya imagine?"

"Even hired killers have some pride. Requiring him to bushwhack me was demeanin'. And then threatenin' a woman was too low to accept. We talked a while before he died tonight and he knew he was dyin'. He wanted to get even with you. He gave me a written statement saying you'd hired him to kill me."

"I don't believe you."

"It's in my saddle bag. I'll get it if you want to see it."

Wally hoped the short conversation had distracted Dooley at least a little. He had practiced the movement McCabe had tried many times but he had always fallen on soft ground and in a frontal movement grabbing his revolver as he started his fall. On this occasion he believed it better to fall backwards grabbing for his gun from an in-flight position hoping his body would drop below Dooey's aim point as Dooley fired his first shot. Dooley only had two bullets and he'd wanted both to count

It happened so fast and yet seemed like slow motion. Wally's knees buckled and he started falling backward. Dooley was afraid to fire too soon or he might miss a falling body or, almost nearly as bad, cause a non-fatal wound. He would wait until the body hit the floor.

He waited too long and Wally's shot, fired just before impact, smashed into Dooley's chest and ended the confrontation.

It was time to contact the marshal.

***

It has now been almost two weeks since Wally's confrontation with Dooley.

Because there were no witnesses to the death of either McCabe or Dooley other than Wally, the marshal insisted on a coroner's inquest.

The delay was caused because the coroner was out of town.

It was a boring wait for Wally, watching Sarah and Adam holding hands and sneaking kisses. He, on the other hand, spent most the day helping the hired hands tend the cattle and the evenings avoiding Helen's sharper and sharper criticism of whatever he did.

There was a bit of news, however. The marshal found a will in Dooley's desk leaving everything he owned to his brother in St. Louis. Through law enforcement there, the marshal was able to advise the brother by wire of his inheritance. The brother immediately responded that he was seventy years old and had no interest in a Montana ranch. He asked the marshal to refer him to someone who would help him sell it. The marshal referred the matter to Arnold Sinclair who approached Adam. Adam and Sarah made an offer.

Finally it was time for the inquest. The marshal testified in support of Wally that McCabe was found on the ground near a water trough on the Clay ranch, a spot where he could fire at anyone coming out the house. Further, his rifle was beside him with one shot fired.

Concerning Dooley, the marshal confirmed that Dooley was found on the floor on top of his Derringer.

The coroner's verdict in each case was self-defense.

And that's what Wally thought they were celebrating when they gathered after dinner in the parlor with a newly opened bottle of whiskey. However, Adam announced, "We all knew what the verdict would be so there's no reason for us to celebrate it. Instead I ask you to celebrate with me the fact that today I asked Sarah to marry me and she said yes.

"Wally, I hope you can stay around for the weddin'."

"I don't think so. Now that I've lost another beautiful woman to another man, I think I'll leave tomorrow for Cheyenne and check out a ranch near my father's place."

Helen spoke up, "It's just like you to give up and run away."

Wally responded, "What do you want? Should I stay here and challenge Adam for Sarah's hand?"

"I'm not talking about Sarah. I'm talking about me.

"Let me tell you a story. It's about a young girl who was self-centered and stubborn. A man she loved asked her to marry him but she was afraid he wouldn't live until the marriage. She asked him if he'd give up being a lawman and go back to ranching. He said he'd just been named chief deputy, the youngest in Cheyenne history. Further he was rumored to be considered by some of the smaller towns around for being their marshal. It appeared to me he loved his job more than me.

"When Jesse asked me to marry him I accepted. Mainly to spite you but also to see if you would change your mind about ranching if I changed my mind about marrying Jesse. You did nothing and you said nothing."

"Helen, you were an engaged woman. What could I do?"

"I'm not through yet. I might have changed my mind anyway but Jesse's father immediately conveyed a hundred acres to Jesse and me as a wedding present and then stocked it with a hundred head of cattle, an instant ranch. This made backing out more complicated.

"All of us could tell in school that Jesse seemed to lack energy, did not join in physical activities. We chalked it up as his being a book worm. His parents didn't tell me he had a serious heart problem and wasn't expected to live long. They wanted him to have as normal a life as possible."

Sarah asked, "Did you love him?"

"I thought that after we married and I got to know him better, I'd learn to love him."

"Did you?"

"Perhaps I would have. He lived less than two years."

Wally cut in, "Helen, it's a sad story so why are you tellin' it tonight when we're about to celebrate an engagement?"

"Because you're about to leave and I want you to know something."

"What?"

"I loved you when you proposed to me and I love you now. You asked me what I want. I'll tell you. If you ride out tomorrow, I want to ride with you. Wherever you go, whatever you do I want to be with you forever. And I think you love me. Do you?"

"Helen, I've never stopped loving you."

"Then what do you want?"

Wally paused, looked her in the eyes, and responded. "If I ride out tomorrow, I want you to ride with me. Wherever I go, whatever I do I want you with me forever."

"That sounds like a proposal and I accept."

"No, no. You proposed first and I accepted.

"Adam, since you'll have Sarah's ranch and likely will get Dooley's, we need to negotiate the price of your interest in this ranch."

"That can wait until tomorrow. Now we'll celebrate two engagements."

Wait," said Helen as she ran to Wally, "if I'm engaged, I should be kissed." Wally pulled her close and kissed her . . . and again . . . and again.

DEATH BY TWOS

Ben Marcus shook his fist in the marshal's face. "You don't seem to want to catch my son's killer. It's been a week now with no progress at all."

"So far," responded Wes Wingate, the marshal of Buffalo, Wyoming, "I have interviewed all Mitch's friends and have been unable to come up with a lead."

"Forget interviewing his friends, talk to his enemies. You know this murder stemmed from the old range war. You can tell by the way it was committed. Mitch was shot and then dragged a hundred feet to a tree just outside the gate to my ranch and hanged. Obvious revenge against me. I think you should bring in Chris Champion. He's still upset that his uncle was killed during the conflict and continues to falsely blame the Wyoming Stock Growers Association for his death. I was a charter member of that group and young Champion has been threatening to hold me personally responsible. This is his way of taking revenge on me."

"You say your stock growers' association was falsely accused of being involved in Nate Champion's death? I'm new here but the word I get is that while several men had Nate Champion pinned in his house, he killed a couple of them who were clearly connected to your group. When the remaining raiders burned down his house and he came out with only a six shooter in his hand, he was filled with enough lead to kill fifty men. Taken together with the written account found on his body as to how he alone defended his home for several hours against an army of invaders, revenge is certainly possible. But you were only one member of the association, so why you?"

"You seem sympathetic to the farmers and small ranchers, Marshal."

"I'm sympathetic to the truth, Mr. Marcus, and my only interest now is to find the killer of your son whether he is connected to the large ranchers or small ranchers, or the farmers for that matter. Keep in mind that although the blood on the ground indicates the shooting took place at the edge of town, my jurisdiction, the hanging took place on a tree in the county, Sheriff Angus' jurisdiction. He's asked for my help."

"I'm advised you intend to question Amy Prescott. Don't."

"It's interesting that you should be concerned. Why shouldn't I?"

"She planned to marry Mitch. She was very nearly a member of the family."

'And now she's not. Did someone want her not to marry Mitch?"

"Just don't question her if you want to remain marshal."

Marcus stomped out of the office.

After Marcus left, Wes leaned back in his chair and tried to remember what he had heard about the "Johnson County War." He recalled it started, as so many wars start, over greed. This was during the open range period in Wyoming. Anyone could graze his cattle on government land and take advantage of its water resources. Further, farmers could homestead the land. This did not please the large wealthy cattle ranchers at all. They formed the Wyoming Stock Growers Association with membership open only the major cattlemen. Using force and intimidation, the large cattlemen attempted to drive off the farmers and small ranchers and keep the water and grazing land to themselves. Hired guns from Texas used lynching based on false allegations of rustling against those who stood in their way. In response, the farmers and small cattle growers formed their own group, the North Wyoming Farmers and Stock Growers' Association. Nate Champion was instrumental in its organization. The war was no longer one sided.

Two events proved instrumental in ultimately bringing the war to an end. One, the shootout at Champion's ranch. After failing to assassinate Champion in his home, a large group of invaders returned late one night and surrounded it. In the morning when two men who spent the night at Champion's ranch went to the nearby Powder River for water, they were captured. Another man, standing in the door of the cabin, was fatally shot. Champion gave as good as he got for several hours until the cabin was set on fire. The fire, more than anything else, upset the locals and shifted public opinion toward the small cattlemen.

When it came pay-back time, Sheriff Angus with a posse of 200 men consisting partly of small ranchers trapped a number of the large cattle growers' hired guns at a ranch on Crazy Woman Creek.

Fighting continued for two days until the raiders were able to get word to the Governor who was friendly to the large growers. The Governor wired President Harrison for help in preventing bloodshed. The President ordered the army from Fort McKinney to intervene and arrest the raiders but the political power of the large growers prevented any convictions.

Enough time has passed now that peace, if not harmony, has returned to the region.

***

Miss Prescott answered the door.

"Marshal, I wondered if you'd come by to see me. You've questioned all of Mitch's friends."

"To be honest with you, Miss Prescott, I couldn't find many. I was delayed somewhat because Sheriff Angus and I had to decide who should question whom. You fell in my group.

"How old are you Miss Prescott and how long have you lived in Buffalo?"

"Why do you ask?"

"It's my job. I'm looking for a killer."

"I'm nineteen and my family moved here five years ago. Other than that, I don't know anything."

"You don't know or you don't wish to tell me. Have you talked to Mitch's father? Did he tell you to remain quiet?"

She looked long and hard at the marshal. Finally she asked, "Martial, do you really want to find the killer?"

"What makes you ask?"

"Mr. Marcus is a powerful man who wields great political influence. Does he influence you?"

"Are you suggesting he doesn't want to find his son's killer?"

"I'm suggesting he's so fixated on Chris Champion being the killer, he doesn't want to risk you finding out he's wrong. He'll be content so long as Chris is hanged."

"You don't think Mr. Champion is the killer?"

"Of course not. I've attended church with Chris for five years now. He is not a killer."

"You seem to think a lot of Chris. What is your relationship?"

"When I first met Chris, we became friends. Then we became good friends. But I live in town and Chris lives on a ranch five miles from town. That prevented a romance from ever developing. Mitch was terribly jealous of Chris, however, and I believe that's why he pursued me."

"You were about to marry Mitch but I don't see you showing a great deal of sadness at his passing."

"Marshal, let me say that while I am indeed sad that Mitch was murdered, it probably saved me from an extremely unhappy life. I didn't love him."

"Then why the marriage?"

"I'm nineteen years old and most of the young women around here that age are married. Chris, the only one I was interested in, showed no interest in me. When Mitch came calling my parents were his greatest supporters. 'Who else is there,' they would ask. 'After all, you're nineteen years old. Mitch is from a wealthy family and he can give you everything.' They finally beat me down and I said yes.

"But I almost broke it off two days before he was murdered."

"What happened?"

"I'm embarrassed to tell you but I will. Mitch behaved very ungentlemanly, totally unlike him. I slapped his face and said if he did anything like that again, I call everything off. He seemed contrite but not surprised and didn't appear overly upset. It was almost as if he wasn't concerned at my reaction. I suspected he may have had another girlfriend who did not draw boundaries."

"How do you know that?"

"Marshal, if I had known he had someone else I would have dropped him long ago."

"Women's intuition?"

"Not really. Intuition is guesswork. Mine is more a feeling, a strong feeling, based on knowing Mitch."

"Does he have a close friend who might know?"

"As you say, he didn't have many close friends. Perhaps Otis White whose parents own the general store. Otis works there."

"Any enemies you know of?"

"Mitch loved to gamble. In school everyone quit betting with him because he would never pay if he lost."

"Anyone else who maybe just didn't like him?"

"How about everyone in town except maybe some of his family?"

The marshal went back to his office scratching his head. He understood why Mr. Marcus didn't want Miss. Prescott questioned. That would have really been some marriage, he though.

***

Wes was in his office writing up his notes on the Prescott interview when Wiley Randolph, Angus' chief deputy, walked in.

"Wes, Sheriff Angus sent me over to tell you Chris Champion is in jail."

"Why is he in jail?"

"That's what Angus wants to know. After the prosecutor met with Ben Marcus, he filed an indictment and insisted Champion be arrested. When Angus asked what evidence Bert had to support the indictment, he responded that filing the charge was his job and getting the evidence was Angus' and your jobs. Angus believes Bert has the spine of a jelly fish and just knuckled under to Marcus. Anyway, you have been advised."

"Thanks, Wiley. Champion is my next one to question. Finding him now will be easy."

Wes met with Champion in a private room at the county jail most often used by lawyers consulting with their clients. The room wasn't being used so the deputies made the room available.

"Mr. Champion, since you're under arrest, you know you don't have to talk to me?"

I know that, Marshal, but maybe you can tell me why I'm here. The county deputies who arrested me apparently had no clue."

"The easy answer is that you have been charged with the murder of Mitch Marcus. I admit the more difficult question is why were you charged, at least at this time. I suppose there are two possibilities."

Wes was interested in getting Champion's response concerning his relationship with Miss Prescott so he asked, "One possible reason is that Marcus was about to marry the woman you love."

"I know you're guessing, Marshal. But I do love her. I thought I concealed that feeling very well."

"Why did you conceal it?"

"Marshal, I'm a rancher without a ranch. I work for my father on his ranch. I have two older brothers in line to inherit and the ranch isn't large enough to divide three ways. I know I will have to move or change what I do for a living in order make my way. What can I possibly offer Amy?"

"Can you think of any possibilities around here for employment?"

"There will soon be an opening as manager of the Wyoming Stock Growers Association. I have been approached by several new members of the group to apply. I know it's because they all hold my uncle Nate in such high regard and my name is Champion. When I remind them Uncle Nate is the one who led the formation of the competing growers' association, they say it doesn't matter. Membership in the original group has been opened to small growers and although the large growers still have the money, the small owners have the controlling vote.

The townspeople still have hard feelings against the rich cattlemen because they had my uncle's house burned while he was in it. Even many of the large growers believe hiring a Champion would improve the image of the association."

"Then it looks like the job is yours."

"Not necessarily. I'm not sure I want it and, anyway, many large and small growers believe I may be too young and inexperienced for the job. If I apply, I'll have to convince them otherwise.

"What is the other possible reason I'm here?"

"Ben Marcus thinks you wanted revenge against him because your uncle was killed during the range war and you blame him. He says you have threatened him and that Mitch's being shot and later hanged at the gate to his ranch shows it was revenge."

"Marshal, I never threatened Mr. Marcus, at least not directly. I have often said I hope they find who is responsible for Nate's death and hang him up. That is a threat to Mr. Marcus only if he is responsible for Nate's death. Mr. Marcus was only one voice, and a minor one at that, in running their group during the range war."

"Do you know of anyone who hated Mitch enough to kill him?"

"Hate is a strong word. Mitch was a bully and ruthlessly picked on smaller boys. I would try to prevent it but I was not always there. Mitch beat Robbie Walker, a much smaller kid, causing him to miss school for a week. Robbie's father went to the prosecutor but either the father or Bert Allen was paid off. Nothing happened."

"Where can I find Robbie Walker?"

"He works at the livery."

***

Wes found Robbie Walker working in the livery and called him. "Mr. Walker, I have a few questions I'd like to ask you about Mitch Marcus."

"Ask away."

144

"How did you feel about him?"

"I hated him. He laid me up for a week."

"Do you know anyone else with such strong feelings against him?"

"At least two. Burl Evans and Tommy Hastings were also bullied by him and were beaten by him a time or two. If it had not been for Chris, we'd all have suffered more from Mitch."

"Did you kill Mitch, Robbie?"

"Marshal, I know how Mitch died. Although I could have shot him, there's no way I could put him back on his horse and hang him. He probably outweighed me by sixty pounds."

"You make a good point. And apparently Evans and Hastings weigh no more than you. But I'm wondering, Robbie, could the three of you manage it?"

Robbie smiled broadly, "You know, Marshal, we probably could have."

"Did you?"

"I'm not going to answer that. That question might help Chris' lawyer show Chris is not the only suspect. After I talk to Burl and Tommy, their answer will be the same."

***

As Wes entered the general store, he remembered the broad smile on Robbie's face as he refused to answer his question. I like that kid, he thought.

Wes saw Elliot White and his wife near the cash register.

"Elliot, I'd like to talk to Otis again about Mitch Marcus' death."

"He's in the storage room, Wes. You can talk to him there."

When Otis saw Wes enter the room, he said, "Marshal. I don't know any more now than the first time we talked."

Elliot White, who had been standing just outside the door, walked in.

"Wes, any objections to me sitting in on this conversation?"

"None at all."

Elliot looked hard at his son. "Otis, you know I never liked your hanging out with young Marcus. I thought and still think he was a bad influence on you. The two of you were thick as thieves. I know you confided in each other. The marshal wants to find out who killed him. Frankly, I don't care if he finds the killer or not. But I care mightily if you don't cooperate with him. Dead men have no secrets. They don't need them. They're well past caring. I will be very displeased, and you will know it, if you don't answer his questions."

"What do you want to know, Marshal?"

Wes decided to explore Amy's "feelings."

"Otis, Amy Prescott said Mitch had another girlfriend and you would know who she is. Do you?"

"That was one of Mitch's big secrets. I guess he told Amy because he knew she would find out he was seeing Maria Alvarez. I know he and Amy had a big argument the last night he saw her. He wouldn't tell me why."

"And who is Maria?"

"She's the daughter of Jose Alvarez, Mr. Marcus' foreman."

"Marcus has a Mexican foreman?"

"Yes and his two sons work with him. Mitch said that Jose knew everything about cattle raising and he and his two sons did the work of six other men."

"Why was Amy bound to find out about Maria?"

Otis paused long enough for Elliot to again intervene, "Answer the question."

Western Short Stories from the Great Northwest

"Mitch got Maria pregnant. Mitch found out about two weeks before his death. She insisted Mitch marry her. She said she wanted to live in the big house as his wife instead of working in the kitchen. He offered her five hundred dollars to go somewhere and have the kid. She laughed at him. When he went to see Amy that last night, he must have thought their days were numbered because Maria continued to refuse a payoff."

"He told you this? What else did he tell you?"

Otis swallowed hard. He looked at this father and then back at Wes. "He said he killed her."

Wes concealed his shock. "When did he do it and how?"

"He met her again in the barn, that's where the often met. They again argued and he shot her. This was the night after he saw Amy the last time. Then in the morning he came to see me. He was highly upset."

"Mitch didn't carry a gun."

"He didn't carry a handgun because he was no good with one. But he did carry a pocket gun like most the professional gamblers. He wanted to have one if those he gambled with had one."

"Why do you think no one has reported Maria's death?"

"That I don't understand since it's been over a week and no one has said anything about Maria's missing. He shot her at night while they were in the barn. He found a shovel and dug a grave behind the barn in a place no one ever visits. He wrapped Maria in a horse blanket and buried her in the grave. I suppose no one has discovered the grave."

"What advice did you give him?"

"I told him to get a lawyer."

***

147

Wes decided to bring the Alvarez brothers in together but question them separately. He sent a deputy out the first thing the following morning before their work day started to bring them in. He decided to question Eduardo, the older brother, first. He might be more protective of his sister. Hector remained in an outer room.

"Why'd you bring Hector and me in? We should be working."

"This shouldn't take long. We're looking into the disappearance of your sister."

"She didn't disappear. She's visiting our aunt in Cheyenne."

"Then that'll make this easy. Give me the aunt's address."

"I don't know her address."

"Will Hector know?"

"I doubt it. Why do you want to know?"

"Because I can have the marshal go to your aunt's home and check on Maria."

"Why would you want to check on Maria?"

"Because we have been reliably advised that Mitch Marcus got Maria pregnant and killed her because she threatened to tell everyone if he didn't marry her."

It was clear that Eduardo was surprised by the new information and highly distraught.

"She was pregnant?"

"Yes. When did you discover that Mitch murdered your sister?"

"I want Hector in here."

Wes had Hector brought in.

"Hector, the marshal knows Mitch murdered Maria. He says Mitch got her pregnant and killed her because she threatened to tell."

The brothers looked at each other and then down.

"Tell him, Eduardo."

"At first we weren't sure. We live in the foreman's house near the barn. Hector was outside the house when he heard what he thought was a gunshot from the barn. He wasn't sure because it was just a pop, nothing like a revolver. He decided to watch the barn anyway. Soon he saw Mitch come out of the barn with a shovel and dig a hole in a weedy section behind the barn.

Then Dad called us to dinner we had to go in. When Maria didn't come home for dinner, Dad became upset and very angry with her. After dinner, Hector told me of Mitch's suspicious activities at the barn.

"We decided to check. We found the shovel in the barn and dug up the hole. There was Maria. We remained calm. First things first. Maria needed a Christian burial. We couldn't do that but we could, and did, rebury he in the Catholic graveyard in Buffalo. We decided on a spot near the edge of the cemetery under a tree. We said all the religious things we could think of. We told Dad that Maria had asked us to tell him she had gone to visit Aunt Rosa. We needed a little time."

Hector added, "We knew we were going to kill Mitch but we argued over who would have the pleasure."

Wes finally reentered the conversation. "What happened?"

Eduardo responded, "We knew Mitch always came home late from town. We waited near the gate to the ranch. We decided each of us would kill Mitch. When we saw him coming, Hector, using Dad's old revolver, shot him out of the saddle. We lifted Mitch back onto his horse and led him to the tree near the entrance gate. Then it was my turn. I tied one end of a rope around a tree branch and the other around Mitch's neck. I hit the horse causing it to run, leaving Mitch dangling there beside the gate."

"You had to eventually tell your father what happened to Maria."

"We did. He didn't agree with what we did but he wouldn't turn us in."

***

Wes, the Alvarez brothers, their father, and their attorney appeared before Judge Shaw two weeks after the Alvarez's arrest for murder. Also appearing was Bert Allen, the prosecutor.

The lawyer representing the Alvarez brothers explained to Judge Shaw in detail the extraordinary facts of the case and suggested a fair plea would be the lesser included offense of manslaughter which carried no more than a fifteen-year sentence.

"What do you say, Mr. Allen?"

"I don't know, Judge. I haven't spoken to Mr. Marcus about it. He's still in shock. I'll need a day or two."

"You don't have it, Mr. Allen. Who do you represent, Mr. Marcus or the people of this circuit?"

"The people of this circuit, Your Honor."

"Well, it didn't look like it when you had Mr. Champion arrested with absolutely no evidence to stand trial for the same murder that's before me now. Mr. Marcus doesn't call the shots in this court. Do you accept the plea agreement or not?"

"Yes, Your Honor."

"Then sign the agreement and let's get on with it.

***

After the Alvarez brothers admitted to killing Mitch, Chris Champion was released from county jail. As Chris walked out of jail, he noticed Amy Prescott waiting.

"Amy, thank you so much for coming to celebrate my freedom. I really appreciate it. I never told you how sorry I was about Mitch."

"Well I'm sorry about his murder but nothing else. I'm extremely grateful to see you released."

"How'd you know to be here?"

"The marshal told me. I suppose because I told him we were very good friends."

"I told him that, too."

"I came by to see you before you rode out of town to tell you that's not good enough. I escaped a horrible relationship and now I want a really good one with you."

"Amy, I'd like nothing better. But nothing has changed. I still have no prospects of supporting you."

"That's not true. You are honest and dependable. You're smart and willing to work hard. People like and trust you. You can't fail to succeed. Those are great prospects. I want to be there in the beginning."

"It seems I have an application to file," Chris said smiling.

POST SCRIPT

The Johnson County War did, of course, take place with the large cattle ranchers fighting the small ranchers and farmers for the open range. The shootout at Nate Champion's ranch took place and he did keep a journal during the final hours. It read, "Boys, I feel pretty lonesome just now. I wish there was someone here with me so we could watch all sides at once . . . Well, they just got through shelling the house like hail. I heard them splitting wood. I guess they're going to fire the house tonight. I think I'll make a break when night comes, if alive. Shooting again. It's not night yet. The house is all fired. Goodbye, boys, if I never see you again."

The siege of the ranch on Crazy Woman Creek where the invaders were surrounded by the sheriff's posse and the intervention by the governor and president happened.

Sheriff Angus, Nate Champion, the governor and the president were, of course, real people acting as indicated. All other characters are fictional.

The end of the range war brought an end to the open range policy of the government.

RODEO WEEK

FACTUAL BACKDROP

Although the story does not feature Seth Bullock, his achievements are important in its development. Bullock, originally from Ontario, Canada, settled in Helena, Montana around 1870. Seth and his business partner, Sol Star, operated a hardware business. When in 1874, gold was discovered in western South Dakota in a gulch filled with dead trees a mining camp was established and called Deadwood. Because of the gold, Deadwood boomed and Bullock and Star moved their hardware operation there to meet the miners' needs. Shortly after Bullock's arrival in Deadwood in 1876, Jack McCall shot Wild Bill Hickok in the back of the head while Hickok was engaged in a poker game. This convinced the Deadwood authorities that a strong sheriff was needed.

Bullock accepted the call to be Deadwood's first sheriff. According to legend, "Bullock's tall stature, broad shoulders and steel gray eyes were so intimidating he could stare down an angry cobra." He brought order to a lawless town. The hardware store flourished until it was destroyed in the great fire of 1894 which burned most of the Deadwood business area. Instead of rebuilding, however, Seth and Sol saw a need in the community for a hotel, and not just a hotel but a large, luxurious hotel. Deadwood had grown so that it was no longer dependent on mining.

New businesses were being started and salesmen were calling on merchants in ever increasing number. The railway had come to Deadwood in 1890.

Another important backdrop is the role cattle played in the region. Cattle ranching was an important industry in Montana and the western Dakotas. In 1884, after his first wife's death, Teddy Roosevelt moved to the Dakota Territory, bought property and built a ranch which he called Elkhorn, and purchased a large number of cattle. He became an active cowboy and even served as deputy sheriff of Medora, North Dakota. While serving as deputy, Roosevelt met and became close friends with Seth Bullock, a friendship that lasted throughout Roosevelt's life.

Cattle rustling became such a problem that cattlemen were having trouble surviving financially. Granville Stuart, after his stallion and 35 head of cattle were rustled, organized a group of ranchers into a vigilante committee similar to the vigilantes that cleaned up the mining camps in Montana. They became known as "Stuart's Stranglers." Through its short existence, the group numbered between 17 and 40 men. They were extremely dangerous and deadly. When they caught a rustler, he was either shot or hanged. A sign would be attached to his chest which indicated either "horse thief" or "cattle thief."

In July, 1884 the vigilantes were tracking down Stringer Jack and his gang. The outlaws crossed the river with some stolen horses and decided to rest in a log cabin not knowing the Stranglers were in hot and stealthy pursuit. The cabin was surrounded and when the outlaws refused to surrender, a gun fight ensued and the cabin was set afire. Although some of the outlaws were able to get in the thick brush and escape, the others were killed, either by bullets or the fire.

Some historians are critical of the Stranglers for their extrajudicial justice meted out without due process of law. Many family members of the victims of vigilante justice agreed.

RODEO WEEK

Seth Bullock, the sheriff of Deadwood, and his deputy, Matt Harding, were sitting in the dining room of the Bullock Hotel which was owned by Seth and his partner, Sol Star. The hotel had steam heat throughout and bathrooms at the end of each hall. It was not the first hotel in the country equipped with indoor plumbing but certainly it was the first in the region. In 1829, the Tremont hotel in Boston and, five years later, the Astor House in New York City, also had indoor bathrooms. And the hotel was large, at least by Deadwood's 1896 standards, with 63 luxury sleeping rooms on the second and third stories furnished with iron and brass beds. On the first floor, there was a large dining room decorated in the Victorian style and a large kitchen, a sample room where salesmen could store their cases, a grand hotel lobby, and offices in front.

"Matt, it's only been a few weeks since I asked you to watch out for my friend, Teddy Roosevelt, when he visited. Now I have another favor to ask."

"Does it involve a mystery like the last time?"

"I certainly hope not. This is a more preventive role. With the Cattlemen's Association meeting here at the hotel in conjunction with the rodeo, I want to prevent matters from getting out of hand."

"I figured that members of the Cattlemen's Association would be older gentlemen who owned rather large spreads and who would bring their wives. That should make them more laid back."

"That would be generally true but there will be some younger fun-loving members among them. Further, many are bringing their foremen and top hands some of whom will compete in the rodeo. These are the ones who concern me. Rodeo time sometimes brings out the worse in people. Also, and this is of some concern, some Deadwood residents remember the activities of Stuart's Stranglers who lynched some of their relatives. Many of these cattlemen coming to town were members of that group."

"So what do you want me to do?"

"Since you're single, I'd like you to move into the hotel during their stay, just be an inhibiting presence among them."

"I don't know, Seth, it'll be hard to take bein' able to go to the privy in the rain and not get wet. It may be hard to go back to an outhouse."

"You can't get over that, can you? The better hotels are putting in plumbing now. Anyway I'll arrange a room for you startin Wednesday."

"I'll pack now."

***

By mid-afternoon the hotel had been filled with cattlemen and their families, foremen and top hands. There were also a few out-of-towners who had come for the rodeo. The hotel was sponsoring a reception in its dining room and, although there was no bar in the hotel, libation as well as food was provided for the reception.

Matt, with his badge prominently displayed, circulated among the attendees. He was stopped by a young man of about 25.

"I'm Junior Donner of the Circle D. You must be Deputy Matt Hardin'. The guy over there servin' drinks says you're a legend around here."

"In what way?"

"He says you're the fastest draw around and you prove it every mornin'."

Matt grinned, "Not on weekends."

"Isn't demonstratin' how good you are showin' off?"

"Like braggin', you mean? I don't look at it that way. I do practice my draw and work on my accuracy most mornin's, weather permittin', and anyone is welcome to attend."

"Well, why isn't that bragging'?"

"Look, I know I'm good and I want others to know it. It may keep them from challengin' me later. I'd rather prove my ability on the practice range behind the jail than on the street. So far it's worked."

"Are you expectin' trouble?"

"No, I'm hopin' my presence will discourage it. The name Donner sounds familiar."

"If you've been in these parts long, it should. My father was one of the leaders of Stuart's Stranglers, a vigilante group that went after rustlers. Although much of the rustlin' took place in Montana, some of the thieves caught were from Deadwood. There's been a lot of resentment for some time. My father still gets threatenin' letters."

"Yeah, I know about the resentment. There's a man here now, Jacob Whittaker who runs a general store, who is still angry after all these years. His brother, seventeen at the time, apparently rode with Stringer Jack's gang when the battle of Bates Point took place. He was one of several men who stopped to rest in a cabin not knowin' the Stranglers knew where they were. The Stranglers set fire to the cabin and several of the men died either from the fire or the shootout. Jacob's brother was one who burned."

"He justifies rustlin'?"

"No, he believes the rustlers should get what they deserve. But he also believes that the accused should get a fair trial and a just sentence. He doubts the death penalty is always appropriate particularly without a fair and impartial trial. I'll have a talk with him in the mornin'."

Matt circulated around the room and introduced himself to various clusters enjoying the hotel's hospitality. Finally he came upon a group in which one man offered his hand and introduced himself as Walter Donner, the owner of Circle D Ranch.

"I just met your son," said Matt. "He tells me you were an active member of Stuart's Stranglers. There is still some resentment here by members of the families of some killed by the Stranglers."

"I can understand that and I'm sorry for those whose family members got involved in rustling. But it had gotten out of hand and put a lot of us in financial jeopardy. And we were effective. After Bates Point, rustling just about ended. But thanks for the tip; I'll stay alert."

Donner turned to a man by his side, "Deputy, I understand the sheriff is a friend of Teddy Roosevelt. Milton Bragg here bought the spread next to the Roosevelt ranch. He also was a leading member of the Stranglers.

"Welcome to Deadwood."

The first day ended quietly.

***

It was a beautiful day for the start of the rodeo which would extend through Saturday. The temperature was moderate, the Montana Big Sky extended across the border and covered Deadwood, the prize money was generous, and the contestants in the early events were outstanding.

Matt didn't see the early events. Instead he visited Jacob Whittaker's general store. He saw Jacob at the counter.

"Jacob, some former members of the Stranglers are in town for a conference of the Cattleman's Association and to attend the rodeo."

"So"

"You've made no secret for you displeasure of the Stranglers."

"I hate them all, if that's what you mean. That's not against the law, is it Matt?"

"Not so long as you don't do somethin' about that hatred."

"Matt, I knew they were coming. It was in the paper. I've been stewing ever since I found out. My wife keeps telling me it was a long time ago and I should get over it. It's not easy but I'm trying. I assure you I won't search them out. But if we run into each other and they confront me, all bets are off."

"Just remember, Jacob, you have a lot to lose."

Matt arrived at the rodeo just in time for the cattle roping event. That's when it happened.

A shot rang out. It was not uncommon when a bunch of cowboys got together, especially at the end of an eventful day, that celebratory shots would be fired into the air. What was uncommon is that only one shat was fired. No one seemed to notice or, at least, pay any attention. No one, that is, except those near Milton Bragg. As Bragg stood up, a bullet entered his forehead and he fell back into his seat. He was dead.

Matt had stationed himself near the members of the Cattleman's Association who sat in the same general area of the stands. He heard the shot and rushed to Bragg. He confirmed that Bragg was dead. asked the cattlemen in the area to stay close by and sent for the sheriff. He then looked around to see which of the cattlemen were present. He also looked to see if Jacob Whittaker was around.

Because of the accuracy of the shot and the fact that it must have been fired at a considerable distance, a rifle must have been used. If a handgun had been used the shooter would have had to be close to the victim; so close, in fact, he would certainly have been seen. Matt looked for a place where a rifle could have been fired without drawing attention. About a hundred yards away stood a horse barn. It would have provided a clear shot at Bragg.

When the sheriff arrived to conduct an investigation of the scene, interview witnesses and provide for getting Bragg's body to the coroner, Matt walked over to the horse barn. There were men working inside the barn who had heard the shot but who had seen no one.

Matt noticed heavy shrubs beside the barn. When he checked behind the shrubs, he found footprints and, more importantly, a shell casing from a .22 cartridge bullet common with hunting rifles. The footprints, although confirming the presence of the shooter, were insufficiently clear to assist in identification.

Matt returned to the scene of the shooting just as the sheriff was finishing his interview with Junior Donner. They then went to the sheriff's office to discuss the case.

"Well, Matt, the interviews of those witnesses who had not left before I arrived were all the same. They heard the shot and saw Bragg fall. I see nothing of particular value. I hope you had better luck."

"I know the spot where the shooter fired the shot; his unusable footprints were there. And I found a shell casing from a 22 caliber rifle. It might help if we can determine who owns such a rifle."

"Probably about every man in town. We can start looking into that tomorrow. Now you'd better get back to the hotel. No telling what might happen tonight."

***

Matt had just gone to bed when he heard two shots ring out. By the time he put on his trousers and boots and strapped on his gun belt, a crowd had gathered around the stairwell at the end of the hall on the second floor. Matt discovered Walter Donner crumpled on the stairs before them.. He was dead from two bullet holes in his chest.

"What happened?" he asked no one in particular.

Mrs. Donner responded through tears, "A man knocked on our door about 10 o'clock saying he was responding to my husband's request to come see him. Walt responded that he had asked to see no one and that the man should leave. Words were exchanged and Walt followed the man out to the stairs where they continued to argue. Shots were fired and Walt fell down the stairs to the second froor."

"Can you describe the man?"

"No, I never saw him. They talked at the door and the man never came into the room."

"Did anyone see who fired the shots?"

"I did," responded Junior Donner. "I came out of my bedroom when I heard the argument. My father was standing on the third floor landing shouting down at someone standing on the second-floor landing. I was near the railing facing my father but I could see down the stairs and see the man but I don't know his name. But I saw him fire two shots up the stairs into my father. If I'd had my gun belt on, I'd have killed him then. When my father fell down the stairs, the man bolted down to the first floor. I heard the night manager ask, "What's going on, Jacob." Then I heard the back door slam as he ran out."

Matt addressed the group, "I ask all of you to go back to your rooms and get some sleep if you can. We'll conduct our interviews in the morning. I'll send for the coroner now and I don't want anyone near the body. Junior, why don't you comfort your mother?"

Matt sent the night manager to notify the sheriff and to fetch the coroner. He then waited by the body.''

***

The following morning was the scheduled business meeting of the Cattleman's Association and, since they could not leave in any event until they heard from the sheriff, the meeting opened at 8 o'clock. First there were various reports to be received and then the election of officers for the next year. They had just finished the elections when, at 10 o'clock, Matt walked in.

All eyes were on him as Matt started speaking, "I express my sorrow and that of the sheriff for the murder of two of your members while visiting our town. I assure you justice will be done."

Someone asked, "Do you have any idea where you might find this Jacob someone?"

"You're talking about Jacob Whittaker and yes we know exactly where he is. He's in jail."

An old bearded man spoke up, "That's good work, Deputy. Now we know justice will be done. At least a dozen of the old Stranglers are here now to see to it. Our verdict is guilty and the sentence is death. We'll take care of justice now and if you and the sheriff get in our way, we walk right over you."

Toby Lockwood, Donner's foreman, spoke up, "Whiskers, those days are over. Leave it to the law."

"Let me caution those of you who might wish to take matters into your own hands. There are two deputies at the jail now with shotguns fully loaded. If they see a mob approach the jail, they will assume you intend to lynch our prisoner. Even without absolute proof of your intent, just like the vigilantes, they will assume your guilt. If you move

162

toward the jail, they will give you vigilante justice and blow your heads off.

"Whiskers, since you appear to be the spokesman for the Stranglers, what evidence did you rely on to return your verdict of guilty?"

"You have to ask? A man later identified as Jacob by your night manager gets in an argument with Donner according to Donner's wife and Donner follows him to the stairs. A witness then sees Jacob shoot Donner twice and then flees the hotel. What is missing?"

"Wouldn't you be interested in hearin' Jacob's side of the story?"

"And you believe him over the word of the wife and the son of the victim? That's the kind of law we got which caused the formation of the vigilantes in the first place."

"It's not important what I believe: it's what an impartial jury believes. Wouldn't you at least like to hear it?"

"I would," spoke up Lockwood.

"Thank you, Mr. Lockwood. I think you'll find it interestin'. Jacob says he received a note purportedly bearing' Donner's signature. It said Donner realized how bad Jacob must feel because his brother was burned alive in the battle of Bates Point. Donner wished to personally apologize and would do so if Jacob would come to his room at 10 o'clock last night."

Whiskers spoke up, "Doesn't that sound sort of fishy?"

"It might, so let's examine it. Jacob had no reason to fear that someone here was trying to set a trap for him. It was his brother that was burned alive. Jacob had done nothin' to cause the old members of the Stranglers to come after him. And he had no reason to believe that he was bein' set up to take a murder rap.

"He was goin' to refuse the invitation, however, believin' that if Donner wished to apologize he should come around to his store to do so. But Jacob's wife got involved. She believed that Mr. Donner had taken the first step and insisted that Jacob take the second. If Jacob did what the note indicated and accepted Donner's apology then the bitterness he has felt for so many years might go away. Foolish perhaps, but wouldn't you agree that wives sometime get you to agree to do foolish things?"

He saw several heads nod in the affirmative.

"Anyway, Jacob says that when the door was opened, Donner asked, "Who are you and what do you want at this hour?"

Jacob responded, "I'm respondin' to your note sayin' you wished to apologize for burnin' my brother to death."

Jacob said Donner looked at him for a minute and then responded, "You must be the one the deputy referred to. I suppose your brother was in the cabin at Bates Point. I agree that burnin' was a terrible way to die and I am sorry it came to that. But he was goin' to die in any event. If he had surrendered he would have been hanged. He knew that and wouldn't surrender. I do not apologize that a rustler met his death. Now go.

"Jacob didn't consider that an appropriate apology and said that since his brother was not given a fair trial, the whole lot of the vigilantes were murderers. That offended Donner greatly and Donner followed Jacob to the head of the stairs sayin' what he thought of rustlers in general, often using foul language.

"Jacob says that when he reached the second floor landin', he heard two shots and thought they were for him. When he saw Donner tumble down the stairs, he knew he had been set up. He ran down the stairs to the first floor, almost runnin' into the night manager, and out the back door."

Toby asked, "How'd you catch him so soon?"

"We didn't. From the back door he ran straight to jail. He turned himself in. He wanted to be protected from you. He said he refused to lose everythin' he had built up by runnin' away from somethin' he didn't do."

"Well, it's his word against Junior's," said Whiskers.

"That's true. But consider this also, Jacob says he never carries a handgun. Think about it. Do any of you know an owner of a general store that carries a handgun? And the night manager says he saw no weapon on Jacob. Peculiar isn't it?"

Junior spoke up, "He could have gotten a gun and carried it here in his waistband."

"I suppose that's possible but highly improbable. Let's consider another aspect of the case. I think we all believe that the one who killed Bragg also killed Donner. I will tell you that at the time Bragg was shot, Jacob and his wife were having a neighbor over for dinner. The neighbor confirms this.

"Also consider this. Although Junior returned in time for his interview with the sheriff, immediately followin' the shootin' he was nowhere to be seen. I checked. I do things like that. Where was he?"

"If you're suggesting Junior killed Bragg, why would he do that? He had no reason."

"I agree you could look for a week of Sundays and find no reason whatsoever for Junior to kill Bragg. And that's exactly why he did it. Junior believed that no one would suspect him for killing Bragg and so if everyone believed the one who killed Bragg also killed his father he'd be in the clear."

"That's crazy. I had no reason to kill Bragg and no reason to kill my father," said Junior.

"Right now, let's stick with the Bragg murder. Our investigation revealed that Bragg was shot with a 22 caliber weapon. When your meeting started this morning, the sheriff went through Junior's room and found a Winchester Model 95 rifle and several 22 caliber bullets."

Junior spoke again, "Sure I have a Winchester. It's a popular huntin' gun. I planned to go huntin' while I'm here. That doesn't prove anythin'."

"Perhaps, but the evidence is beginnin' to mount.

"For example, I was delayed today because I was meetin' with the coroner. He has interestin' testimony to give. He says Junior is lying through his teeth, or words to the effect. He says that by alignin' the entry and exit wounds in Donner's body you can see conclusively that the fatal shots were fired on the same level as Donner and slightly to his left. This analysis places the shooter on the third floor in the exact position Junior admits to havln' been.

"I admit I can't figure why Junior would kill his father but provin' motive isn't necessary."

Toby hesitated to respond but then stated, "I may be able to help you there. Mr. Donner confided in me a lot. Under the circumstances, I believe Mr. Donner would want me to tell what I know. Things were not well between father and son. Mr. Donner believed his son had no gumption. He had no interest in growing up and taking responsibility. He told Junior he had to be out of the house by the end of the month and that he was going to disinherit him. He made it clear to Junior that he would have to earn his way back into his estate. It's possible Junior found that more challenging that merely killing his father before the will could be changed."

Mrs. Donner glared at Lockwood, "Toby, you should not have disclosed a confidence shared with you by my husband. You'd better look for another job."

"Evelin, your son murdered Bragg and he murdered his own father." I'll find another job before I work for Junior."

Mrs. Donner faced her son, "Junior, say it's not true."

"Mama, you know he hated me. He was throwing me out of the house and taking me out of his will. What else could I do?"

Matt looked at Whiskers, "I'm curious. Here you have the son of a member who has just confessed to murderin' two former members of the Stranglers. As a former Strangler are you willin' to apply vigilante justice to one of your own?"

The old man looked down and walked quietly back to his room.

A BODY, A BULLET AND A MYSTERY

Art Hinkle, having arrived in Buffalo, Wyoming ten minutes earlier from Helena, had entered the Cattlemen's Saloon to meet his fellow agent, Ray Holland, dispatched here two days earlier. Ray's job was to see if Tom Horn was actually in Johnson County and, if so, where. It was a meeting no one knew about or should have known about. He was seated at a table away from the bar having a beer when a man approached him with his hand on the butt of his still-holstered gun and a look in his eye suggesting he knew more than he should about their looking for Horn.

"Stand up, Cowboy," he ordered.

Art stood up.

"What's your name, Cowboy?"

"Well, I guarantee you it isn't Cowboy."

"I didn't ask you what your name ain't. I'm goin' to assume it's Hinkle and you're a rustler. I think we need to see which of us is faster with our gun. Let's step outside."

"You, sir, have the wrong man. I'm not a rustler. In any event, I admit you're faster so there's no need for us to step outside. I just wear this gun belt because people tell me it's manly. When you're as skinny as I am, six foot two and a hundred sixty pounds, you need something to make you look manly. Besides I'm not very fast. In fact, people measure the speed of my draw with a calendar. I can hit the broad side of a barn at twenty paces but then there's little demand for that."

Actually Art wasn't telling the truth. A stop watch determined it took him two and a half seconds to draw and fire three shots. This was faster than the outlaw sheriff of Bannack, Montana, Henry Plummer, who was lynched by the vigilantes for secretly leading a band of road agents. Plummer was reputed to be able to draw and fire three shots in three seconds. In fact, Art stands in the company of Bill Hickok, John Wesley Hardin, and Billy the Kid as among the fastest gunmen in the West.

This conversation was interrupted when Art saw Ray being prodded through the saloon door by a man with his gun drawn and pointed at Ray's back. He was now standing about five feet behind Ray whose back was to him just inside the saloon door.

"I got one, Steve. He was in the livery askin; too many questions and responded to the name of Ray Holland. Who are you talkin' to?"

"My man doesn't want to give his name so my guess is we have both of them. Let's take them out in the street and get rid of these two rustlers. Skinny here says he's no good with a gun and I believe him."

Art asked, "Why do you think we're rustlers?"

"We heard two men by the name of Hinkle and Holland were coming in to meet up with Tom Horn. That's all the evidence we need."

"But during the range war Tom worked for the cattlemen."

"Tom's loyalty easily shifts. Word has it he's now working for sheep men and our boss doesn't think he needs you two to help him."

"Ray, it looks to me like Cheyenne all over again."

This provoked Ray's attention that he should be prepared for anything. Art was facing the side of the man holding his gun on Ray. Steve was facing him with his hand still on his holstered revolver. To test Art's theory of delayed reaction which he had argued extensively with Ray during their recent trip to Cheyenne, he needed to neutralize

Steve. In order to distract him, Art lied. "Thank goodness, the sheriff just walked in. He'll want proof we're rustlers."

Then, as Steve quickly and predictably turned to look at the saloon door, Art vigorously kicked him just below the knee with his hard, sharp-toed boot. He watched Steve grab his leg in pain and fall to the floor with his revolver sliding several feet away.

Art commenced his draw as soon as his toe connected with Steve's knee. Steve grabbed his leg and started screaming in pain. Art was over half through his draw when the other gunman looked his way.

[One thousand and one, one thousand . . .]

Art could feel the barrel of his revolver clearing his holster.

This image of Art drawing his weapon was sent to the gunmen's brains which processed the information and signaled he was facing danger. The brain works fast but not instantaneous. Because Art's action was unexpected, this signal took about 0.7 of a second.

[and two, one th . . .]

Art's barrel was now lining up on the gunmen facing Ray.

The gunman's braisn instructed him to turn his gun from Ray to Art, another 0.2 of a second.

[. . . ousand and . . .]

The men facing Ray started to swing around.

There was no appreciable delay in the time it took for the bullet to fly from Art's gun barrel and smash into the chest of the gunman holding Ray and drive him to the floor.

Steve was still writhing on the floor as Art and Ray left the saloon with everyone looking curiously at them. Outside, Art whispered, "My horse is in front of the hotel. I'll move him to the livery and join you in your room. We need to talk."

Art soon joined Ray in his hotel room.

***

"I know we discussed your idea of delayed response time while we were in Cheyenne during our last assignment. But I still don't understand why the man with his gun pointed at me didn't just swivel and shoot you dead when you started your draw."

"Ray, you know I had a year in college before my money ran out and I joined you at the Pinkerton agency. In one class, they talked about "reaction time" which is the time required for the brain to process information newly presented to it. For example, assume I'm walking down a path holding a loaded rifle to meet a friend to go hunting and, turning a corner, I run head-on into a bear charging me from about ten feet. My brain will recognize this aa a threat but not immediately. Because I didn't expect a bear to be there, it will take most of a second to alert me to the danger. Once I am aware of the danger, there is a further delay in determining what to do. Should I jump out of the way, run like the blazes, or raise my rifle and shoot? To physically take any action will also take time. In this case, the bear wins. If I had expected the presence of bears on the trail, my reaction time would have been about two tenths of a second and I may have survived.

"In our case since the gunman was primarily watching you, I figured on being half way through my draw before he noticed me. I figured it would take him at least a half a second to realize danger from an unexpected source and then additional time to determine what to do and then physically do it. If I can't win a shootout with all this time as a head start, I should be shot."

"It was awfully close. Why'd you take the chance?"

"I didn't consider it taking a chance. I thought of it as taking advantage of the only chance we had. They were going to take us outside and shoot us. If they got us outside, we'd have no chance."

"Anyway, I've decided I don't want to participate in any more of your scientific experiments."

"Nor do I. Steve, of course, presented a different problem. He was facing me with his hand on his gun-butt. He was alert for any action I might take and his reaction time would be much quicker. I had to distract him momentarily and I did that by saying the sheriff was entering the saloon. When he turned toward the saloon door, I kicked his knee out of joint and removed him as a problem."

"Well, I don't understand it but it worked . . . this time. How do you think they knew we were coming?"

"I would guess a local slip. As you know, we're here to meet a large rancher who was glad to see the range war finally end and doesn't want to see a new one start, this time between cattlemen and sheepherders. When he heard Tom Horn was back in the area and knowing Horn has occasionally worked for Pinkerton, he contacted us for advice. Our agency is embarrassed to have employed someone with Horn's reputation so we're here to offer any advice we can. Probably someone connected with that rancher, Joseph Ward is his name, is responsible, intentionally or not, for our greeting today. We'll visit Mr. Ward in the morning."

***

Joe Ward responded to the knock on his door.

"Come in, gentlemen, you must be from Pinkerton."

"Yes. I'm Art Hinkle and this is Roy Holland. We were told at the agency that you have concern that Tom Horn may incite another range war and we were asked to discuss your concern with you."

"Well, he may have already incited one. Willie Nickell, the four-teen-year-old son of Kels Nickell, a rancher who introduced sheep into the area, was found shot dead on July 18. Kels and a cattle rancher, Jim Miller, have been feuding over Miller's allegation that Kels' sheep were grazing on Miller's property. Horn visited the Millers only a few days before Willie was found dead. Shortly before Willie's murder, Kels was wounded and several of his sheep shot or clubbed to death. Jim Miller and his son were arrested for this but released on bond. Horn wasn't around when Kels was shot so he may be clear of that. The Millers' arrest, however, may have made them more cautious when it came to killing so many think they hired Horn to do what they tried to do earlier. My concern is that sheepherders and cattlemen may take sides in this feud and the matter get out of control. That's why I contacted Pinkerton. It's no secret Horn has worked for your agency from time to time. I believe him to be the lowest form of life. He seems to be proud that he's killed seventeen men for money and I doubt any of these men were facing him."

"If Horn does become involved, won't it be on the cattlemen's side? Aren't you a member of the cattlemen association?"

"I was a founding member. But we got involved in the first range war to stop rustling. We did that but we didn't always conduct ourselves nobly. At the time, we believed our actions not only justified, but necessary. We were overrun with rustlers, far too many for individual ranchers to manage or the law to handle. So we had a meeting and decided to collectively take the offensive. We organized, hired some gunmen from Texas, and went after the rustlers in a big way. At the time, we had the support of the public. We were applauded for getting rid of rustlers. Then it got out of hand. I'm afraid our gunmen killed too many small ranchers with no proof they were rustlers. Public opinion changed. I resigned from the association."

Art responded, "Our agency admits to having hired Horn in the past; he's an outstanding tracker and we were unaware of his other shortcomings at the time. What do you want us to do?"

"Just get Horn out of here before all hell breaks loose."

"Before we leave, I have another question. We were greeted today by two men who wanted to kill us as rustlers because someone told them we were here to meet with Horn. I have no doubt they intended to kill us, but the reason given could have been a cover. What do you think?"

"Feelings are running strong since the killing of the young son of the sheep rancher. If another range war comes, both sides may want to hire Horn. He's that good. Someone may want you to stay out of it."

"Do you have any idea where we might find Horn?"

"My ranch hands say that if Horn's around, he often spends his evenings at the Angry Bull Saloon."

***

That evening, not expecting it to be so easy, Roy and Art visited the Angry Bull. After about thirty minutes, they saw Horn enter with another man and head toward the bar. Some in the crowd referred to Horn's companion as "Miller."

Horn stopped half way to the bar and waived Miller on.

"I see some old friends. I'll see ya' later."

"I imagine your visit to Buffalo is to see me. You have a message from Pinkerton?"

Art responded, "A request really. A lot of our clients in this area are afraid you might be involved in the start of a new range war which they don't want. Pinkerton hopes that based on our past relationships you'd be willing seek employment elsewhere. By the way, do you know why we were met by a group of men who wanted us dead?"

"I've heard a rumor that someone from Pinkerton may be thinkin' of comin' in on the sheep ranchers' side. But I think you're wrong,

Slim, about unrest. The cattlemen, large and small, are getting' along fine. I know of no problems at all."

"How about trouble between sheepherders and a particular cattleman, say the gentleman you came in with?"

"I don't know what you mean?"

"I mean the murder of the fourteen-year-old Willie Nickell. I met with the sheriff today. It appears both you and Miller are suspects in that case. It might be a good time to go to Texas."

"Slim, you know if I'm a suspect it's no time to flee. That might be an admission of guilt. Besides, I've heard of no evidence against me. They can't convict on speculation."

"The murder has all the earmarks of a Horn killing. A shot from a rifle, no boot prints at the scene of the body matching yours, no hoof prints which can be tied to your horse, and no eye witnesses who saw you do it. It may indeed be the method of the killing that ties it to you."

"You think it was a long distance shootin'?"

"Tom, you were a tracker for Pinkerton, and a very good one. Also you were very good at bringing in the men you tracked. But I am a detective for the agency. It's my job to determine who should be brought in."

"Okay, Detective, why should I track myself?"

"First, why do I believe it was a long-distance shooting? The answer is because of who the victim was, a fourteen-year-old kid. Tom, I just don't think you'd kill a kid even for a lot of money so why'd you do it? The answer that comes to mind is that you didn't know you were doing it. Miller is not reputed to be a great rifle shot particularly at a substantial distance whereas that's your specialty. At a distance of say two hundred yards you could easily mistake the youth for his father. A long-distance shot explains why you left only a body, a bullet and a mystery at the scene.

"The real reason why I believe it's you who killed the kid and not Miler is that Miller is a cattleman who knows little about killing while you're an expert, coldblooded killer."

"Now, Slim, I think that was intended as an insult. I believe you want me to demand satisfaction and insist we go outside and shoot it out at twenty feet. I might do that with some people but not with you. You'd shoot me before I get my gun out of the holster. But I think I'll kill you anyway. Certainly not up close and not when you'll expect it. It'll be a surprise and it'll be painless and with no boot prints, no hoof prints, no witnesses and, like you say, only a body, a bullet and a mystery found at the scene." Tom Horn rose and walked to the bar.

***

Horn was summoned to the door by a loud knock. Suffering from a hangover, he responded slowly and with little enthusiasm.

"What the hell do you want at this hour?"

"Mr. Horn, it's almost noon. I have a problem to be solved and you come highly recommended. When I mentioned my problem to you last night at the saloon, I was told to come by your room today. However, based on your current condition, the job may be beyond you."

"What's the job?"

"I want a fellow removed but it won't be easy. He usually travels with a group so it will take someone who is accurate at long distance with a rifle. I will pay well but there will be only one chance so I have to be sure I get the right man."

"If I agree to take the job, I'll be the right man."

"Are you accurate at two hundred yards?"

"I just shot that young sheepherder from three hundred yards; it was the best shot I ever made. Who do you want killed?"

"I'll get back to you."

Horn's visitor was not looking for a man to do a killing, he was looking for a man who had done a killing, specifically the killing of the son of a sheepherder. The visitor's name was Joe Lefors and he was a deputy marshal.

Horn was arrested the next day and this hungover confession was used against him at his trial in which he was found guilty and sentenced to death. Horn's appeal was denied.

Art wet to visit Horn shortly before his execution.

"Tom, for what it's worth, I think you were wrongfully convicted. Oh, I believe you killed the boy but I fear the deputy embellished what you said. I think you'd brag about the shot but I don't believe, even drunk, you'd say you knowingly shot the boy. Somehow fairness seems to balance out though since you had many other murders which went unresolved."

'Somehow that's not very consolin', Slim. But with me gone you're off the hook. I wasn't goin' to kill you anyway. I don't like to work for nothin'."

Horn was hanged in Cheyenne without giving up the names of those who had hired him either during the unrest between cattlemen in the Johnson County war nor for killing the boy.

POST SCRIPT

Reaction time, the time that elapses between when a person is presented with a stimulus and the person initiating a response to the stimulus, has long been of interest to the psychologist and scientist. Mental chronometry is the use of response time in perceptual-motor tasks to infer the content, duration, and temporal sequencing of cognitive operations. In other words, to indicate how fast the individual can execute the mental operation needed by the task at hand.

Sir Francis Galton and Franciscus Donders were active in this field in the mid-1800s.

Mental chronometry is now often used in accident reconstruction to determine how long it took the driver to respond to an emergency situation—a deer in the road or a truck running a stop sign and pulling into his path. The reaction time has been found to be roughly 0.7 of a second for all normal persons which suggests the reaction time depends on some basic aspect of the human psychology – involving the brain, nervous system, and muscles – which does not vary much from person to person. Would a slower reaction time indicate impairment?

Some tests involve anticipated stimulus such as shouting or pushing a button when the participant sees a green light flash. In this case, the participant knows the light will flash at any time but not just when. The reaction time in these cases is roughly .2 of a second.

Concerning the account of Tom Horn, this story is, of course, fiction but Tom Horn is not. Horn had been a scout, an interpreter, a tracker, and a hired killer. He is reputed to have killed seventeen men for hire. Art and Don do not exist and any conversation involving them did not take place. A conversation did take place however between Horn and Deputy Marshal Joe Lefors and, although perhaps different from the one set out in the story, the content appears similar. Lefors testified at trial that Horn admitted shooting from a distance of 300 yards, his best shot ever, and that killing the boy was the dirtiest trick he had ever done.

PROF SMITH

Charles M. Harris

Joshua Smith had been on the trail two days to reach Cheyenne and had spent last night in a bedroll along the trail. A few years ago this would have been normal, even enjoyable. With the passage of time, however, his forty year old bones protest. Adding to his misery is the gunshot wound to his shoulder which has not fully healed but simply could no longer delay this trip.

He had to find a place for his horse, a comfortable room for himself, a bath, a shave, a quiet drink and a good dinner. Now, having accomplished all of these except the drink, he entered the Cattlemen's Saloon.

He noticed several men clustered at one end of the bar loudly celebrating someone's birthday. Josh settled at the other end and ordered a whiskey and was about to move to a side table farther away from the party.

"Hey, Mister. We're celebratin' my twenty-first birthday. Come join us."

"I thank you but I've had a long day and all I want now is a drink and a good night's sleep. Barkeep, the young man's next drink is on me. Happy Birthday."

"My name's not 'young man.' It's Chester Holland and you're jus' puttin' me off. That's rude and no one's rude to Chester. Get down here now."

"Kid, I told you I'm tired. Don't push me."

"You called me 'kid.' Rude to me a second time. Just so you'll know who you're talkin' to, my father is high up in the Wyoming Stock Grower's Association. You don't know how powerful they are and my father, Will, is one of their leaders."

"That's amazingly ironic."

"What's ironic?"

Josh knew the youth's brashness was getting under his skin but he couldn't resist.

"Well, Birthday Boy, you've asked a single question which might be interpreted in two ways. First, you may be asking what it was you said that I find ironic but that would indicate some smarts. I believe instead you merely want to know the meaning of 'ironic.' That you can look up."

"That's all the insults you get away with."

Chester stepped away from the bar and squared up.

The barkeep looked at Josh. "You look vaguely familiar. Many years ago I was a barkeep in Virginia City and I'm wondering if you're the one they used to call Prof?"

"Some used to call me that."

"Chester, don't mess with him or he'll kill you. His friends called him "Prof" because he had some college but what he was known for was bein' a quick draw and a deadly shot."

"I don't care what he was then; look at what he is now. He's old."

One of Chester's friends celebrating his birthday added, "Leave him alone, he not botherin' no one."

"All right, I won't shoot him if he'll toast ne now with the drink in front of him. What do you say, Mister?"

Josh looked at him slowly. Surely not, he thought, doubtful that this old trick was still being used. It was never very successful.

"Chester, I drink to you," he said reaching for his glass.

Josh kept looking into Chester's eyes. When Josh's hand neared his glass, he saw Chester go for his gun. Josh ignored the glass and drew. Long ago, he had actually practiced this move and found that if he acted immediately drawing second had no appreciable effect on his draw. He pulled the trigger while Chester's gun barrel had not cleared his holster. The bullet smashed into Chester's elbow before Chester could get off a shot.

Chester looked in shock at his damaged arm. "My father will get even with you for this. If you're not gone by tomorrow morning, you'll be seein' him."

"That's the irony I was talking about. I came here to see your father. Tell him I'll be having breakfast at the café around the corner at about eight o'clock."

"You should know, Old Man, my father has recently hired a man faster than you, Chad Wilkins. He's probably as old as you are but I would imagine Dad'll bring him along.

* * *

Josh knew Chad well. At one time they had been very good friends. They went hunting and fishing together. Even double dated. While in their twenties, they served as deputies in Deadwood. Josh had gone on to marshal a small town in Wyoming and Chad had moved to Virginia City where rumor has it he used his gun indiscriminately, working for mine owners guarding gold shipments during good times and doing less savory jobs when the gold started drying up. It was only a rumor because no one could identify Chad as doing anything illegal.

Three years ago Josh married and moved to a ranch in northern Wyoming. Circumstances, and Will Holland, changed all that and now Josh is here looking for revenge.

* * *

Actually Will Holland was no longer a leader of the Cattlemen' group although he wanted people to believe he was. Three months ago, Holland showed up at Josh's ranch to make him an offer. He introduced himself as a leader of the Cattlemen's group knowing Josh had only recently joined. Josh knew that Holland held no office in the Association and was not held in high regard.

They were standing out near the corral in front of Josh's ranch house when Holland made his pitch.

"Smith, you are reputed to be the fastest gun in these parts and since I need a fast gun, I have a proposition for you. You know the price of beef is way down. I need to raise some capital fast or I'll lose my ranch. I have four ranch hands who can help but they need a leader for the job. I've just found out the Merchant's bank in Cheyenne will be loaded with cash Friday. I, with your help, will take it."

"Why do you think I'd do somethin' like that?"

Because you and Chad Wilkins are good friends and the two fastest guns in Wyoming. You've both left law enforcement and I know you must have fallen on hard times operating this ranch with the drop in the price of beef. The banks are just waiting to take advantage of the bad market and take our ranches. And I know that Wilkins is not particular about what he does so I figure you may not be either. I wouldn't have asked you if I wasn't desperate. Wilkins operates out of Virginia City and you're almost local. I figured I'd try you first.

"The deal is this. A banker friend knows I'm having financial problems. There's a major deposit coming into his bank next Friday. It will arrive on the afternoon stage and no additional security is planned. We can either hit the stage as it comes into the depot or hit the bank after the money is taken there. I figure my four ranch hands with a seasoned gunman such as you will have no trouble. We split one third to the banker, one third to me and a third to you. I will take care of my ranch hands out of mine. It's a lot of money for all of us. What do you say?"

"I'm amazed you'd think I'd accept and surprised you'd take the chance of askin' me. What's to keep me from notifyin' the law?"

"I considered that possibility but I hoped it would work with you. But you notice no one is near us and anyway no one here has even seen me. You're unarmed. This is what will keep you from notifying anyone."

Holland drew his revolver and fired. The bullet hit Josh in the shoulder and knocked him to the ground. On hearing the shot, Josh's wife came running out of the house. Holland turned his weapon on her and fired. When the ranch hands came running from the barn, Holland, believing Josh was dead or dying, turned and fled.

Unfortunately for Holland, Josh's wife died but Josh did not. He was in the hospital for a week before anyone gave him a chance of recovering. It was three months later when he walked into the saloon in Cheyenne and encountered Chester Holland.

* * *

Josh went to his scheduled breakfast and assumed Holland would appear. He expects some of Holland's men, perhaps his old friend

Chad, will also come. He arrived at the restaurant before it opened and looked around the exterior of the building. There were three doors, the front, the back and a side entrance leading out of the kitchen to the garbage area. This door was not apparent from the customer section of the restaurant and could easily be missed by someone sent to watch the rear.

Josh knew his chance of surviving a shootout with Holland and his men was slim. But he wasn't here to survive. He was here to kill Holland. If Holland did not join his men in the encounter, then Josh needed a chance to escape to find him. This door presented a long shot. But it was a chance.

At eight o'clock the restaurant door opened and Chad walked in . . . alone.

"Where's Holland and the rest of his men?"

"I told Holland I wanted to talk to you without him or his men. They stayed at the ranch. Holland says you hate him but won't say why. You know as fast as you are, you can't succeed in killing Holland with me here. Why are you so determined?"

"I'll admit you make it more difficult but not impossible. We never decided which of us is faster. I hope you will understand that in this case even attemptin' to fulfill a commitment to myself is as important as achievin' it. I have to try."

Josh described his initial encounter with Holland in which his wife was murdered.

"You mean I was Holland's second choice?"

"I've often wondered how I would do facin' you. When I watched you draw back in Deadwood it was like lookin' at myself draw in a mirror. As a kid that's how I practiced. I saw you make the very same movements. I'm sorry I have to find out which of us is faster before I kill Holland."

"I'm not here to kill you today. To be honest with you, I thought about shooting you in the arm so you couldn't go after Holland but after hearing what Holland did to you, I think you deserve a chance at him. I told Holland about just shooting you in the arm and he said it probably wouldn't work. He said you'd just wait until you healed and then come after him when I wasn't here. I now know why that concerns him. I'd try to talk you out of it but now I see how difficult that would be. I know I'd do the same."

"Chad, doesn't this remind you of when we were deputies and would meet to plan our actions when we knew we would be facing a shootout?"

"Yeah. But then we were on the same side. When ae you coming out?"

"I plan to come out to his ranch in the morning, probably about eight."

"Please, Joshua. You're the closest friend I've ever had. Just go home."

With that, Chad walked out.

* * *

Josh got to the ranch long before sunrise. He scouted the area around the ranch house and amazingly found no evidence of guards. He saw the kitchen and dining area jutting out from the main house. About thirty feet from it was the bunk house. It was a flat-roofed building with the walls rising a couple of feet above the roof providing Josh a small area of concealment. A tree near the building gave him easy and silent access to the roof. He climbed up and waited for sunrise.

Finally the sun started to rise. He could hear activity in the bunk house and could imagine Chad dressing and buckling on his holster.

Further down, he could make out Holland in the main house, buckling his gun belt and leaving his room. The cook had coffee going in the kitchen and Holland headed there. He shortly stepped out of the kitchen to see if his ranch hands were getting ready for Josh's arrival. This was going to be a remarkable morning. But not for Holland.

Josh could hardly believe it when Holland stood thirty feet from where he was kneeling. He would not waste this opportunity. He fired, hitting Holland near the heart. The ranch hands and Chad came running up. Holland looked at Chad and said accusingly, "You got the time wrong. You said he wouldn't fail to be here at eight. You owe me Smith's life."

"What I said was he wouldn't be late. I didn't say he wouldn't come early. But you're right; I did let you down. I'll kill him and you can count on it."

Holland was beyond hearing the promise.

Chad looked around, "Anyone have any idea where the shot came from?"

Josh answered, "Yes, it came from up here." Josh was covering Chad and the ranch hands with his revolver.

"What now?" asked Chad.

"Get rid of the ranch hands and I'll come down. No sense endangerin' them."

"I agree." Chad sent the hands to the bunk house and ordered them to stay out the way.

Josh climbed down the tree and faced Chad with his gun holstered.

"Josh, you came a little early and I'm not talking about this morning. I stuck around here only because Holland had one more robbery planned. Otherwise I'd of been gone. If this one is as successful as the last, I'll be a rich man and retire."

"And do what?"

"To be honest, I haven't considered that. If you survive what will you do?"

"I don't know; I just killed a man for revenge. I can't go back into law enforcement. I was a terrible rancher and without Iris I wouldn't try it again."

"Why didn't you try to escape?"

"Even if I got away I know you'd follow me. I heard you give your word to Holland that you'd kill me and I know you'll try to keep that promise. I'd rather get it over with now.

"I regret this, Josh, I'll miss you. When you're ready."

They went for their guns. Indeed they were mirror images of each other. Even the sounds of their gunshots could not be distinguished from each other.

Josh felt the bullet enter his chest. His knees buckled and he fell to the ground. So this is what it's like to lose, he thought. But then he saw Chad also on the ground with blood coming from a wound in his chest. He started to crawl toward Chad.

"Why're you coming over here?" Chad asked.

"I don't want to die alone."

When he reached Chad he could see he was dead. He tried to touch Chad's shoulder but his hand fell short. Josh's eyes closed and the eternal darkness set in.

END

Printed in Great Britain
by Amazon

37583263R00109